Poked

Kelly Cheek

Cover and book design by Kelly Cheek

ISBN: 978-1-7335022-2-1

Fiery Muse Publishing
Littleton, Colorado 80129

Printed in the United States of America

Facebook people are finding me that I don't really know. People poke you on Facebook. I'm like, "Why? Why are you poking me?"

Bridget Kelly

At 1340 Pennsylvania Street, in Denver, Colorado, stands a stately stone house which was once the home of Denver socialite and philanthropist Margaret Brown. Known as Maggie throughout her life, she only, inexplicably, became known as Molly after her death. This home and museum, still furnished with many gaudy items that once belonged to the woman of unsinkable fame, is surrounded by other opulent historical homes.

Less than two blocks north of the Molly Brown House is Colfax Avenue, a 26-mile long street that bisects Denver and its suburbs. In the distance of a block and a half, the buildings at Pennsylvania and Colfax are decidedly less opulent.

In a dark and musty basement apartment facing an alley in one of these buildings sat Elliot Logan. The only illumination in the old, squalid apartment was a forty-year-old desk lamp outfitted with a forty watt bulb, and the twenty-five-year-old computer that Elliot Logan was hunched over.

Elliot was a self-proclaimed computer geek who, at twenty-two years old, had accomplished quite a lot. His profound affinity and expertise with all things electronic had earned him a reputation in many diverse circles, including a few branches of law enforcement.

Though not always on the favorable side.

Having been called up on a couple of high-profile hacking charges a few years back, he had chosen to turn state's evidence and help the police catch the people who had hired him. In a short time, he earned a reputation, and now helped them on a consultant basis. If a case involved computers, and the tech department of the Denver or other local police departments couldn't figure it out, Elliot was often the one they called.

Elliot's features were soft and attractive, boyish even, with fair hair and skin. His blue eyes were a little large for his face, which he liked to say was because he was a nocturnal creature. The dark circles that usually underscored them added credence to that claim.

His features were further hardened a bit by his usually disheveled hair and his rumpled clothing. Since the majority of his time was spent in front of his computer, in the privacy of his own dingy apartment, he didn't see the need to dress up.

He had lost the ball that screwed on to the end of the circular barbell he wore in his left earlobe, and he hadn't had a chance to get another one. In its place, he had shoved a paper clip through the piercing. After two weeks, it was still there.

He sighed, sat back and stretched. Then, picking up his stained ceramic mug, he went to the coffee maker and poured the last of the coffee. He turned the coffee maker off and winced as he took a sip of the sludge that had been sitting on the burner for too long.

He would have preferred a glass of bourbon, but it was three o'clock in the morning, and he wasn't finished with his work, yet. He needed the caffeine.

He tilted his head both directions, popping his neck, took another drink of burned coffee, and sat back down at the computer. He rubbed his eyes and looked at the screen.

Elliot barely remembered his father. He had only seen him a few times, and that was when he was a toddler. Yet here Elliot sat, working into the night, poring over twenty-year-old documents with the aim of clearing his father's name.

Tony Logan had been a private detective in New York City who got in a little over his head. Ryan Flanagan, the head of an Irish crime family in Queens, had been the target of Tony's last investigation. Tony was getting close to being able to prove Flanagan's guilt in a number of smuggling cases. Before he could wrap it up, though, the FBI arrested Tony for suspicion of involvement or complicity in the Oklahoma City bombing.

Elliot had vague memories of his mother bringing him to Denver for the trial. Most of what he knew about it, though, he had learned later.

Tony maintained his innocence throughout the trial, held in a different court room, but congruent to the much more publicized trial of Timothy McVeigh. He knew nothing of the evidence that the FBI found on his computer, but the evidence was damning. Tony was found guilty and sentenced to twenty years in ADX Florence, the same supermax federal penitentiary that Terry Nichols would also be remanded to.

Elliot was five years old when his father's twenty year sentence began. But Tony was killed only a month into his prison term, apparently by an inmate, but nobody could determine or prove for certain who was responsible.

Elliot looked at the computer screen and took another sip of the burned sludge. He put the cup down and shut the computer off. He needed to sleep.

Forty-five minutes due west sits Georgetown, Colorado, a picturesque little town nestled in the mountains off I-70. Once a silver mining camp, the 1.2 square mile town now made its primary living from summer tourism. During the summer months, its roughly two block long downtown area, lined with western storefronts and surrounded by Victorian-era homes, swells with people looking for a day away from the city.

Not far from 'downtown' Georgetown stood a funky little cottage built right between the dirt road and Clear Creek. The interior of the cottage closely followed the contours of the exterior, with slanted ceilings over rooms and narrow hallways, and with unexpected little alcoves serving as display areas for ceramic pots or a vase of dried flowers.

In her bedroom, Valerie York was stirring. She always woke up early, an irritating hangover from her previous life. It's not like she had to clean up after a drunken husband anymore, but internal alarms, like old habits, die hard.

Valerie got up and showered. She spent a few minutes brushing the tangles from her blonde hair, but she didn't bother drying it. She donned blue jeans and a sweatshirt, and she left her room. She stopped outside Shannon's door and quietly opened it, and she saw pretty much what she had expected.

The room was empty. Aside from all the clutter and the dark imagery plastered all over the walls.

Valerie sighed and closed the door, making her way down the steep narrow stairway.

Shannon had been such a sweet little girl when she first came to live with Valerie. At five years old, children are resilient. Shannon barely remembered anything about the accident that had killed both her parents.

In her kitchen, Valerie selected a little plastic K-cup and fitted it in her Keurig coffee maker. She filled it with water, placed her cup in the recess for it and while it started brewing, she went out the front door and picked up the newspaper. She didn't pay that much attention to the world news. The world was a mess, and there was nothing she could do about it. Local news affected her more direct-ly, and she sometimes had a little influence over that.

Although she usually felt helpless in the face of what happened right in her own home.

Valerie's brother, Peter York, had been a successful Denver entrepreneur with an uncanny business sense, and with his fingers in lots of different pies. He had money to burn, but he was also generous and had been happy to use some of it to help Valerie get set up in her new life after she divorced Bill fifteen years ago.

The years of mistreatment she had endured at Bill's hands, both physically and emotionally, had made a mess of her psyche. It had taken a lot to finally get her to take the step of moving out and divorcing him, but Peter was more than happy to help. She initially moved in with Peter and his wife, Kristy, and at Peter's suggestion, began seeing a therapist to help her work out the issues resulting from her time with Bill.

Then, when she felt strong enough, Peter helped her get set up on her own, in Georgetown. It had felt good putting that distance between her and Bill, but she was still within a comfortable driving distance to the city, and to Peter.

Moving out on her own, her life had changed drastically at that point. But two years later, when Peter and his wife were killed in a car accident while on their way to visit her, she realized that she hadn't really known what change really was.

Valerie inherited the bulk of Peter's fortune, and their five year old daughter, Shannon, who had been strapped into the back seat and survived the crash.

The silver lining had been that she didn't have to work. Peter's portfolio contained a good balance of stable and high-yield investments. Valerie lived simply and was able to do so comfortably on the interest alone. Having become a bit of a hermit, this suited her lifestyle very nicely.

The Keurig noisily squeezed the last of the coffee into Valerie's cup, and she picked it up and went out her back door, onto the deck. The creek was rushing past, carrying spring snowmelt down from the high country, and Valerie sat down to listen and sip her coffee.

What else could she do?

Pennington Clark placed some blue jeans in the suitcase that was open on his bed. For the first time in years, he was taking a vacation. A real vacation, not just a weekend up the North Shore. All the years he had worked as an art director at ImageWerx, a Boston design studio, he had never taken an actual vacation.

Years ago, when he was a graphic designer, it had been easier for him to get away. But after he had gradually built a reputation as one of the most sought after designer/illustrators on the east coast, followed by his promotion to senior art director, he became almost indispensible, to the point that a day or two at a time was all he could manage.

He pulled a few t-shirts out of his dresser, and when he closed the drawer, a picture on top wobbled momentarily, catching his eye. Shelley. He still hadn't gotten rid of the photograph.

Shelley Sellers was an exuberant brunette with intense green eyes. She wasn't quite beautiful, but she had a striking appearance, and Penn was attracted to her from the moment he first saw her. She was a freelance artist who occasionally did some work for ImageWerx, and their similar creative interests had given them something to talk about for a few dates.

But Penn was not a conversationalist. Shy and tongue-tied, he had spent most of his life alone, pursuing his own creative interests, seldom interacting with other people. A natural introvert, he always welcomed common interests when attempting to converse with someone.

When Shelley first spent the night with him, he realized that they shared another interest. She was an intense lover – exciting, adventurous, and nearly tireless. Penn found that when conversation failed him, there was always the bedroom. Or wherever the mood struck. In a short time, they had made love in every room in his home and hers. Within a couple of weeks, she moved in with him.

Penn turned away from the photograph and put the shirts in his suitcase. He didn't want to think about Shelley again.

Their year together hadn't been bad. Not all of it, anyway. In fact, she had lasted longer than other relationships he'd had. But their lovemaking, as good and exciting as it was, wasn't enough to base a lasting relationship on. Their time together eventually became dull, she got bored with him and they called it quits.

She hadn't been around for a couple of months now. She stuck around long enough to help him with the transition from ImageWerx art director to work-from-home free-lancer.

But now she was gone.

Now that he had finally taken the plunge and was on his own, he was able to make his own schedule, to the extent that the deadlines allowed. He had been fortunate that a number of big clients from his time at ImageWerx followed him when he went freelance.

Living alone again, he was able to focus his free time and his creativity into once more being one of the most sought after designer/illustrators. He was also becoming lonely and isolated, and that was partly what influenced his decision to take a vacation.

Penn had never been to Colorado but had always wanted to go. Now that he had both the money and the time, he was taking advantage of a connection he had there.

A connection he had never met.

A few years back, he had become online friends with a Denver art director through Facebook, Arden Chase. During their time on the social media site, they had swapped sob stories and encouragement. Their situations had been sadly similar.

About a year ago, Arden had inadvertently made a break from his ad agency, and was now happier than he had ever been. Encouraged by that, but knowing that 'his mileage may vary,' Penn sat down and did some figuring, and some conversing with clients.

He had determined that his chances of survival were good enough to take the leap of faith. That had been four months ago, at the beginning of the year.

Now, still able to afford groceries, and the mortgage on his Back Bay brownstone, he decided that it was time for a vacation.

Penn closed the suitcase and put it on the floor at the foot of the bed.

He climbed the stairs to his fourth floor studio. Sitting down at his computer, he checked his e-mail. He had done an FTP transfer a half hour ago, the last illustration he had scheduled before his vacation. His e-mail now contained a message that the client had received it and everything was good to go.

So was Penn.

He quit all his applications and shut down his computer. He stood up and looked out the back window, northward across Storrow Drive to the Charles River. He had always loved this view of the river, with Cambridge and MIT beyond.

Now, he was looking forward to a different kind of scenery.

JuleighAnn Harper stretched and opened her eyes when she smelled coffee and bacon. She looked beside her in bed. Arden wasn't there, and she was just sitting up when he entered the room carrying a tray.

"Breakfast in bed?" she asked. "Arden Chase, what did you do?"

"What do you mean, 'what did I do'? I made you breakfast in bed."

She looked at him through narrowed eyes, as he put the tray down across her lap.

"You're not trying to butter me up for something?"

"I am thoroughly offended at the distrust and suspicion that's being leveled at me."

JuleighAnn smiled as she looked at the tray. An omelet, with bacon, toast, orange juice and coffee. She looked at Arden with raised eyebrows.

"You know, if you really are doing this without an ulterior motive, you've raised the bar quite a bit for what I'm going to expect from you in the future!"

"Well actually, there *is* something I kind of want you to do." JuleighAnn tilted her head and looked at him with an

'I told you so' expression. He went around to his side of the bed and sat beside her. Then he made a show of being uncomfortable and wrestling something out of his back pocket. When he pulled his hand back, it was holding a paperback book. "I've found this great new author that I think you'll enjoy. I'd like for you to read his book."

JuleighAnn took the book from him and looked at it. The cover looked like something on a typical romance novel.

"Since when do you think romance novels are great?" she asked.

"The genre doesn't matter if a story is told well."

"*Green Eyed Lady*, by Dean Arches?" She looked at Arden. "Never heard of him."

"Which part of 'new author' did you not understand, my dear?"

She rolled her eyes and looked at the back cover.

"Two star-crossed lovers battle against impossible odds," she read, using a melodramatic voice, "spanning time and space to be together. Is their love strong enough to survive their struggle, deep enough to stand the test of time?" She looked at Arden with an 'I don't believe this' expression. "What made you think I might even *possibly* like this?"

"I just had a feeling," he replied nonchalantly. "Your breakfast is getting cold."

JuleighAnn sighed and took a bite of her omelet. As she chewed, she opened the book to the beginning of the story.

"It was a dark and stormy night," she read. She looked at Arden again with a grin. "This isn't for real, is it?"

Arden looked offended and got up, feigning an emotional upset.

"Okay, you're just being impossible," he said. "I know you like to read, and I thought you would enjoy this story. I was trying to do something nice for you, but if you just can't bring yourself to try something new, then I'm going to go downstairs."

"Alright, princess," JuleighAnn said condescendingly, "I'll read the book."

Arden continued down the stairs, grinning to himself, as JuleighAnn turned her attention back to the first page.

> It was a dark and stormy night. As the wind howled outside, Augustine Smith felt his heart quicken in his enormous, muscular chest when the crowd parted and he found himself gazing into the lustrous, emerald eyes of Gillian, the sienna-haired goddess standing before him.
>
> "You may call me Gus, milady," he said with a chivalrous bow.

Now there was a familiar name! When JuleighAnn first met Arden online, he was going by the name Augustine Smith, or Gus, in a fake Facebook identity. She looked back at the author's name. Dean Arches. She smiled as she real-

ized it was an anagram for Arden Chase. And once she noticed that, she could also see the similarity between her
own name and that of Gillian, the heroine of the story.

All but forgetting about her breakfast, she was now
grinning as she continued reading.

Denver International Airport was a big place, its total land area almost double the size of the island of Manhattan. It was listed, in 2013, as the fifteenth busiest airport in the world with over fifty-two and a half million passengers. The distinctive tent-like roofline of its main terminal, made of white Teflon-coated fiberglass fabric, was alternatively likened to the nearby snow-covered Rocky Mountains, and to the teepees that once dotted the high plains.

While a boarding pass was necessary to get past the TSA security lines and into the concourses, the main terminal was open to anyone.

Shannon York split off from her two friends and they slipped into the crowds of people moving to and from the concourses. The eighteen-year-old was at once distinctive and forgettable. Her black hair, clothing, eyeliner, lipstick and nail polish, as well as multiple piercings, made her stand out from the crowd in general. At the same time, it all distracted and drew attention away from her actual facial features.

She was actually pretty, but few people recognized it. She considered her dark accoutrements her real features. But she was happy to take advantage of the disguise capability they offered.

However, Shannon was good at what she did. She usually didn't have to rely on such distractions.

Earlier in her short life, Shannon had been what her aunt Valerie would consider a good girl. Orphaned at five years old, Shannon had accepted Valerie as her family, essentially a substitute for her mother, though Valerie never tried to assume that position.

But Shannon had been marked by her experience. Shortly after the accident, the nightmares started. Or rather, she had the sense that it was a nightmare, but she couldn't remember anything disturbing about it. It always started out with her and her parents in the car, but that was all she ever remembered.

It was assumed that it likely involved the accident but, never being able to remember anything beyond that scene, they could only make assumptions based on how she felt afterwards. Valerie did what she could to help Shannon sleep more soundly. Doctors and prescriptions had helped a little, but the dreams never went away completely.

In her teens, the goth subculture started attracting her. Though true goths might reject her and her friends as poseurs, she immersed herself in the look, loving the almost 'undead' quality that she was able to achieve. She felt comfortable in the darkness, and in the disguise.

When she started slipping into illegal activities with her friends, she was happy to hide behind that disguise, and to take advantage of the shock factor that it supplied.

Now, in the airport, she moved with the flow of the foot traffic in the terminal, always on the lookout, ready to act whenever she saw whatever she was looking for: a wad of cash, a gold Rolex, a diamond bracelet. She wasn't particular.

Perfect! she thought, as she saw the man in front of her. A shoulder bag hanging at his side, he probably thought it was protecting the wallet in his back pocket. In fact, though, Shannon knew that she could use the proximity of the crowd, and the sensation of the bag bouncing against him, to cover her snatching the wallet.

She matched his speed, peripherally watching others around her, as she inched closer. The man was blissfully unaware.

Shannon, however, was just as unaware of the airport security guard following her. Until she slipped the wallet out of the man's pocket. At that moment, one hand grabbed her arm, and another grabbed the shoulder of her victim.

She tried to break away and run, but the guard held her too tightly.

"Shit!" was all she said.

Hunter Sage sat in a dumpy little coffee shop on East Colfax Avenue, near downtown Denver. Hunter was in his thirties, but gave the impression of someone older, not because of his features, but because of his countenance, his demeanor. In his past as a cop, then as a private detective, he had seen things that had left a mark. Not the least of which was the brutal murder of his wife nearly four years ago. That had left many unseen marks, and a couple of visible ones in the form of scars on his wrists from his failed suicide attempt.

It was nearly noon, and Hunter had been up for several hours. He looked toward the counter where Elliot Logan, his client, was waiting for his order. Elliot was a late riser, and this was breakfast for him, so even though Hunter was ready for lunch now, he nursed what he considered a late coffee.

Hunter had moved to Denver from North Carolina just a few months before, and his internal clock still had not been reset to Mountain Standard Time. It had been a difficult decision, but one which, ultimately, had been for the best. Aside from that unattained temporal adjustment, though, he liked the area. He missed the south, but Colorado had a lot to offer.

He took a sip of his coffee, which wasn't as bad as he expected when he first saw the place. The geeky kid skulked toward the table, carefully drinking from his cup as he walked, carrying a folder under his arm, and a cinnamon roll that didn't quite fit the plate.

"How's it going, Hunter?" Elliot asked.

"Going fine, Elliot," Hunter replied with his southern drawl, watching the kid with a little bemusement. Elliot didn't look like the stereotypical kind of geek that, at twenty-two, was still a virgin. Hunter thought, instead, that he looked more like the stereotypical Hollywood hacker, pierced and tattooed, living on coffee and sugar. Still an introverted geek, but on the cutting edge of being hip, or cool, or sick, or whatever the kids called it nowadays.

"Had any luck?" Hunter asked.

"A little," Elliot replied, his eyes not quite open yet. "I was up till about three o'clock going through my old man's computer, and I've found a few files that might be useful."

"That's great!" Hunter said. "Because I managed to convince the FBI to reopen the case."

"Really? Dude, that's excellent!" Elliot's eyes opened a little with that news.

"Yeah, but that's on the condition that the evidence warrants it. So we need to present them with a pretty convincing case."

"We'll have one, man." Elliot pushed a folder across the table toward Hunter. "Here's a sample of what I've found."

Hunter opened the folder and looked at the printed sheets. E-mails dating back to the early 90s, they were mostly sent to an old AOL address for Tony Logan. Skimming through them, Hunter saw numerous references to Ryan Flanagan, the Irish mobster in New York. Correspondence with overseas suppliers, bills of lading tying him to potentially illegal shipments of art and antiquities, accusations from a disgruntled former employee.

And there was one particularly interesting e-mail detailing Flanagan's desire to have Tony Logan out of the way. The message was sent to someone called Rayzor Blayd.

"Rayzor Blayd?" Hunter asked.

"He was an elite hacker," Elliot responded, leaning forward, a little more animated now. "His real name is Jerry Fulton, but some hackers take on names that kind of become their trademark. Rayzor Blayd started hacking on the old USENET systems in the 80s, then adapted to the internet in the 90s."

"A hacker? You'd think Flanagan would be talking to one of his enforcers."

"This makes perfect sense," Elliot said. "Considering that evidence was found on my old man's computer tying him to the Oklahoma City bombing."

"So you think this Rayzor Blayd hacked your daddy's computer and planted that shit on it?"

"Yeah, man, check the date." Hunter looked at the date on the e-mail. April 25, 1995. "An anonymous tip was called in to the FBI on the twenty-ninth, and my dad was arrested."

"So in the four days in between, this hacker planted false evidence on Tony's computer, then reported him to the feds."

"My old man knew what he was doing. He was a geek himself. He wasn't elite, but he was a pretty damn good hacker. That's how he was able to intercept that e-mail to Rayzor Blayd. He wrote his own encryption protocols, too, and used them to hide those e-mails there."

"Yeah, but encryption in the 90s?" Hunter interjected. "Computer encryption was still relatively primitive back then, wasn't it? Wouldn't the FBI have found this?"

"They didn't bother to look. The false evidence wasn't encrypted. It was right there in the open. Right on the desktop, I think. Once the FBI found that, they stopped looking. No way Dad would have been that careless.

"Besides, his encryption was advanced, especially for the 90s. It's been days since you convinced the FBI to re-lease his computer from their archives. It's taken me that long to break his encryption so I could get to those," he said, motioning to the folder.

"Well, son," Hunter said, "you told me you had *a little* luck. I think this is a lot more than a little. Whether it's enough to put Flanagan out of business or not, I don't know. But I think we definitely have enough for the FBI to reopen your daddy's case and potentially clear his name."

*Z*ounds!" Augustine exclaimed. "What mounds!" He unceremoniously wiped the drool from his mouth as Bertha, the chamber maid, stepped out of the last of her petticoats, dropping them on top of the pile already on the floor.

"Well, ain'tchoo just a sweetiepie!" she said as she flipped her blonde hair over her shoulder, causing her bounteous breasts to bounce in a most abrupt and breakneck fashion. "This here endowment is all fer you, darlin'. Why don'tcha come and git it!"

"Madam, I am most humbled and appreciative of your generous, erudite and, indeed, attractive offer," Gus said, struggling to still the quiver in his voice, and to quell his burgeoning loins, "but alas, my heart belongs to another."

JuleighAnn shook her head, smiling as she continued reading *Green Eyed Lady*, the book Arden had given her. It was such a ridiculous story, switching back and forth from absurdly overdone southern accents to old English-style prose. It was as if a weird time and space warp had occurred, mixing a gothic romance with Li'l Abner.

And she was surprised that the story didn't include a time and space warp.

Yet. She was early in the story and realized that there was still plenty of time for Arden to throw that device into the mix as well.

But she recognized it as a bizarre retelling of their account, the story of how Arden and JuleighAnn had gotten together, and she was enthralled with Arden's creativity. He had come back to the bedroom a couple of times to check on her before she had finally finished her breakfast, long since gone cold.

JuleighAnn had reluctantly taken a few minutes to get up, get dressed and brush her teeth. Then, she went downstairs, carrying the book with her, poured another cup of coffee, and joined Arden on the rear deck. He looked up at her, smiled, then returned to the newspaper, acting as if he had no interest in whether she was reading the book or not.

Molson was down in the yard, sniffing around near the chain link fence, occasionally looking up as one of several pairs of ducks paddled by on the lake. As they disappeared behind the cattails, the Golden Retriever resumed his sentinel duties.

JuleighAnn had just opened the book when her cell phone rang. She sighed and put the book down, then looked at the caller info on the phone. She tapped the green receiver button.

"Hi Valerie," she said. "How are you?"

"Hello, JuleighAnn," Valerie replied. "I'm fine, thanks. Listen, I was wondering if Shannon and I could come and see you sometime soon."

"Professionally, you mean?" JuleighAnn thought about the coming week. She was taking a couple of days off for the visit of Pennington Clark, Arden's friend from Boston. As a result of that, on the days that she *was* working, she had scheduled back-to-back visits to the hospitals where she consulted as a grief counselor.

"Yes," Valerie replied. "It's about Shannon." JuleighAnn thought her voice sounded tight, tense.

"My schedule is kind of crazy for the next week, but I just had an idea." She looked at Arden who was still reading the paper, as she continued. "We're having a barbecue tomorrow afternoon. Why don't you come over for that?" Arden looked up at her, and though JuleighAnn wasn't quite sure what his eyes were saying, she had a pretty good idea.

"Are you sure?"

"Absolutely! After we eat, Shannon and I can go in my office and talk privately."

"JuleighAnn, I appreciate that. Thank you so much!"

"Not a problem," JuleighAnn replied, still closely watching Arden's eyes. "Four o'clock."

After she disconnected, Arden spoke up.

"So, Marilyn Manson's coming over for dinner?" His sarcastic edge belied the forced calm in his voice.

"She's a sweet girl," JuleighAnn said in a placating tone. "She's just troubled."

"We should probably hide our valuables," Arden mused, unfazed by JuleighAnn's response.

JuleighAnn just sighed and picked up her book.

"Well," Arden said, glancing at his watch, "I'll leave you to your literary amusements." He gathered up the sections of the paper and neatened them into a stack.

"I just got out here and you're leaving me?"

"I have to get ready to go to the airport. Penn's flight lands in a couple of hours. Besides, I think I'd only distract you from your highbrow occupations," and he nodded toward *Green Eyed Lady* on the table in front of JuleighAnn.

"Yes, I *must* be able to concentrate to follow the complex story that Mr. Arches has crafted!"

Arden scooted his chair back and gathered up the paper. Then, he stood up and leaned over JuleighAnn's chair, kissing her softly on the lips. JuleighAnn put her hand along the back of his neck, holding him there and prolonging the kiss.

"It was a clever attempt," Arden said when he was finally able to stand back up, "but you'll not deter me from my mission. I must away to the airport."

"I love you, Arden," JuleighAnn said with a warm smile.

"I love you too, honey," Arden replied, his sardonic façade crumbling before her.

Grounded, Shannon sat on her bed, brooding. She scrolled through the playlist on her iPod, a score from cruising Denver's 16th Street Mall a few months ago. Some people were so careless! With the ear buds in her ears, she located the track she was looking for, Intestinal Crank by Cannibal Corpse. She hit 'Play' and clipped the iPod to the sleeve of her black t-shirt.

As the churning guitars began their staccato attack, Shannon allowed her dark eyes to sweep around her room. They alighted on the corner of a laptop computer, partially hidden beneath the clutter on the floor of her open closet. The computer was another score from the airport just the day before.

She got up and pulled the computer out of the closet and placed it on the bed in front of her. She pressed the power button and waited for it to start up. She had looked at it after she got it home, but had not been able to get in, due to the password protection. Now, though, she was prepared. She hoped.

She pulled a flash drive from the drawer of her bedside table, and slipped it into the USB slot. One of her friends had acquired a password cracking app and gave her a copy of it. The gRam Cracker startup screen replaced the computer's password window, showing the cheesy drawing of a graham cracker 'plugged in' to the side of a computer. The application was designed to start working automatically, and indeed, once the startup screen cleared, the 'brute force' program began trying possible passwords.

Shannon knew it could take a while, so she set the computer aside and sat back against her headboard, to continue brooding.

The ride home from the airport that morning had been a long one. Valerie was pissed, but hardly said anything. At least Shannon hadn't been arrested, but the airport security people were almost as despotic as the police. Maybe even more so. Rent-a-cops were such self-important pricks, always so full of themselves.

Shannon wasn't looking forward to tomorrow. Valerie told her that she had arranged for them to visit JuleighAnn Harper, the therapist that both she and Valerie had visited on occasion in the past. That part wasn't so bad. She knew that JuleighAnn was cool. At least she *tried* to understand Shannon. But the idea of sitting through a barbecue with a bunch of old farts didn't appeal to her.

They always looked at her like there was something wrong with her. The piercings and black makeup were meant to shock. That was the point, and she felt as if they served her well when she was 'working the crowd.' Crowds were impersonal, generic.

But up close and face to face, she had to deal with how people felt about her.

Shannon often felt guilty about her relationship with Valerie. She knew that Valerie loved her and was concerned about her well-being. They had been closer when Shannon was younger, as Valerie worked through her issues dating back to her shitty marriage. Over the years as Valerie's confidante, Shannon, without realizing it, had absorbed Valerie's feelings about men and relationships.

A couple of years before, there had been a boy at school that Shannon liked. But he had been cruel to her, which seemed to reinforce those negative feelings about men. After a while, she started feeling this way about other friends and acquaintances too. In one way or another, most people just didn't seem to measure up.

Though she would never admit it to Valerie, the sessions she had with JuleighAnn when she was younger had had some effect on her. She was fascinated with the inner workings of the mind and made a private analysis of it. By now, she had studied psychology enough to know that the problem was largely her own. She was pretty and had a keen sense of humor, but she felt inadequate, likely having absorbed those feelings from Valerie as well.

And she projected these feelings onto others, imagining that everyone else thought she was inadequate, too.

In time, she had altered her appearance so that most people who saw her would find her unattractive. Some even reacted with a visible repugnance. In this way, there was no conflict between how she felt about herself and how others saw her. It helped to vindicate her own personal feelings.

She had changed reality to match her perception of it.

Having found a few friends who shared her view of the world, they supported each other in their rebellious pursuits, at which Shannon proved to be gifted. But she knew that Valerie supported her too, and wanted to help her walk the 'straight and narrow.'

The straight and narrow just wasn't any fun.

Her gift came with a price, though. She felt guilty. While it didn't seem to bother her friends, Shannon felt a nagging pang of remorse every time she stole something. Valerie had taught her right from wrong, and Shannon knew which side theft was on.

The lesson was tenuous, but it was still there.

She heard a bell tone from the computer and she pulled it closer, glad for the distraction from the guilt feelings. And there in front of her was the desktop. The program had found the password already, and Shannon made a note of it for future reference.

Now, it was time to begin exploring.

owdy, Red," Hunter said as he came into the kitchen from the garage and closed the door behind him. Kenzie looked up at him from the potato salad she was making, and she smiled. She loved the assortment of pet names he called her, especially uttered with his southern accent.

And to think she used to not like southern boys!

"How did it go?" she asked.

Hunter dropped his keys in the little brass bowl on the end of the counter, and placed the folder of Elliot's printed e-mails next to it.

"Really well," he replied. "I think we got more than enough to convince Ed to reopen the case." Ed was his contact at the FBI. Hunter usually referred to him as J. Edgar.

"That's great, honey," Kenzie said as she wiped her hands on a towel. She melted against Hunter as he wrapped his arms around her.

Attracted to the sound of Hunter's arrival, Jarvis came into the kitchen and wrapped himself around their feet as they embraced. Jarvis was an orange tabby, formerly the pet of his late wife, Kathy. Hunter was never a cat person, but Kenzie loved Jarvis, and the feeling seemed to be mutual.

"Mmm, that looks good," Hunter said, looking over Kenzie's shoulder at the big bowl of potato salad.

"Yes, it does. But it's for the barbecue tomorrow, so you can't have any." She smiled up at the chastened look on his face. He appeared to want it even more, now.

But seeing her face in front of him was enough to draw his attention away from the potato salad. Held in the glow of Kenzie's warm brown eyes, Hunter often forgot what he had been thinking just moments before. Those eyes seemed to see past the pain and anger that had afflicted him since the brutal murder of his wife, Kathy, nearly four years earlier. Now, Kenzie's eyes could find the happiness that he had buried and bring it to the surface.

Looking at her smiling face, Hunter was, as always, powerless to resist. He smiled back at her as he tightened his embrace, and he crushed his lips against hers. Kenzie moaned softly, feeling his hands in her luxuriant red hair, the inspiration for his most recent pet name.

Reluctantly, he pulled away from her and looked at her again.

"You know, sweet thing, if I wasn't so hungry, I just might take you upstairs and have my way with you."

"If I wasn't so hungry," she replied, "I just might let you." She pushed him away with another smile. "Go relax. We can eat in just a couple of minutes."

"Oh yeah? What do you have in mind, li'l darlin'?"

"When I was frying bacon for the potato salad, I made a little extra. I'll have BLTs ready in just a bit."

"Mmm!" He looked at her through narrowed eyes for a moment, then nodded as if reaching a tough decision. "Yeah," he said, "I think I'll keep you."

Kenzie shook her head and smiled, gazing into Hunter's eyes.

"I love the way you smile," he said, taking her in his arms again.

"Yeah, the corners of my mouth turn up and everything," Kenzie retorted.

"Not just your mouth, smartass," Hunter said, returning her smile. "When you're happy, you just get it all over your face."

"I *am* happy, honey," Kenzie enthused. "I've never been so happy!"

Beaming at each other, Hunter let go of her and sat on one of the stools at the bar while he watched Kenzie assemble the sandwiches.

"One of these days," he said, "I'm gonna get you to try a possum, lettuce and tomato sandwich."

"Sure you will," Kenzie replied with a shake of her head, but not entirely sure if he was kidding. Then she looked up at Hunter. "Do you miss home very much?"

"My home is with you, baby," he said softly.

"Oh," Kenzie said, in a high, drawn-out tone that women reserve for things that touch them in a particularly romantic way. She paused while she looked at him, and

Hunter silently congratulated himself for saying exactly the right thing. "But you know what I mean," Kenzie continued. "Do you miss Allure?"

"No, honey, Allure is a shithole. But yes, I know what you mean. Yeah, I miss North Carolina. I even miss my stupid brother."

Hunter's brother, Parker, was the one that Kenzie met first, on Facebook. Though they were both married, they fell in love, and Parker eventually coaxed Kenzie out to North Carolina. He backed out at the last minute, though, opting to try to work things out with his wife, Lily. But everything turned out well when Hunter showed up to break the news to her. The mutual attraction was almost instantaneous.

"Have you heard from Parker lately?"

"Not much," Hunter replied. "Couple of text messages. You knew Lily let him move from their guest room back in to their bedroom after we moved here." Kenzie nodded. "Sounds like they're doing alright. Lily's in a much better frame of mind, and it sounds like they're falling in love again."

After Kenzie's emotionally charged history with Parker, being in the same proximity, but now with Hunter, just seemed weird to everyone involved. Since Kenzie missed Colorado and her friends, Hunter agreed that it might be best to make a move.

"That's good," Kenzie said, finishing up the sandwiches. "I'm happy for them."

"I am too," Hunter said. "But I think I got the better deal."

Kenzie looked up at him and shook her head again, and she sighed.

"I think I did too."

"I do miss possum, lettuce and tomato sandwiches, though."

Kenzie sighed.

Shannon was poking around on the stolen laptop, but she wasn't finding anything that was terribly interesting. She hadn't necessarily expected any kind of high-tech proprietary software, though it would have been nice. Instead, it was all pretty standard stuff – Microsoft Office products, iTunes, Skype. There was a program that looked as if it was meant to copy DVDs. That was cool.

She saw the Chrome browser pinned to the taskbar at the bottom of the screen and she started it up. The first page that came up was Facebook, already logged in to an account for someone named Don Lewis.

"Thank you, Don," Shannon said, "for making it so easy for me."

She went to Don's "About" page and saw that the previous owner of the computer was a balding man, forty-six years old, he lived in Ketchum, Idaho, and judging by some of the photographs, he had a real love of various kinds of weaponry. There were photographs of knives, swords, guns of all kinds, and several photographs of Don himself posing with an assortment of weapons. And a couple of photos of electric chairs.

"Shit! You're a real ray of sunshine, Don."

There wasn't much personal information about him, but he did include a couple of favorite quotes.

> Just vengeance does not call for punishment. – Pierre Corneille
>
> Revenge is an act of passion; vengeance of justice. Injuries are revenged; crimes are avenged. – Samuel Johnson

Shannon scrolled further down his "About" page. She didn't recognize any of his friends. She didn't figure it was likely they had mutual friends. He was a member of a few Facebook groups, but none that she had heard of, or that interested her in the least. A couple of gun groups, one for vintage weapons enthusiasts, one called "Swift Poker." She was already growing tired of him.

"Sorry, Don," she said. "You're a real downer!"

She logged out, then logged into her own account.

That's better. People she knew. Some she liked. Some, not so much.

Roger Kenley fell into the latter category. He was a guy up in Wyoming, some conservative asshole in Cheyenne. Shannon couldn't even remember how or why she ever connected with him, but he was getting to be so irritating! He had sent her numerous personal messages, and he often had something to say about status updates she posted. He usually disagreed with the viewpoints she expressed, sometimes quite rudely.

And now, he had sent her another personal message.

"Shannon, I saw your picture of the new piercing you got. Why do you do that to yourself? You used to be so pretty! You're just fucking up that beautiful face!"

She had three rings in each earlobe and one through her right eyebrow, a Monroe piercing above her lip to the left, and now a curved barbell through her septum, the one that Roger was commenting on. While Shannon did catch the *sort of* compliment in his message, overall she was just irritated by his judgment of her. She was tired of him.

She moved the cursor over his name and hovered there until the drop-down menu appeared, selected "Unfriend," and then she breathed a sigh of relief. It always felt good to rid herself of assholes.

If only it was that easy in real life!

She saw a notification that a friend had poked her. She had been exchanging pokes with a friend she'd never met in real life, Kevin in Portland, Oregon, for several weeks, and the tally was up to 759. She returned the poke, liking, as always, the vaguely sexual connotation to it.

After browsing her notifications for a few minutes, she left Facebook and went into Tumblr, where she had a number of friends. But even that was boring. She was sick of being stuck in her room.

She really needed to get a car! Being eighteen and grounded was particularly irksome. She was an adult. She should be allowed to do what she wants!

She was glad that Valerie was around when Shannon needed to be picked up at airport security, but still . . . .

She pushed the computer away, sat back against her headboard and sighed.

Pennington Clark stretched his legs out on the passenger side of Arden's BMW. He had toyed with the idea of flying first class, but he hadn't quite been able to justify it yet. So after the cramped quarters on the plane, it felt good to have a little more leg room.

"And nobody knew that Augustine Smith wasn't a real person?" he asked, smiling, as Arden recounted his exploits with a fake Facebook identity the year before, leading up to meeting JuleighAnn.

"Well, I had a couple of close calls," Arden replied, "but in general, I was able to keep it up for a couple of weeks. I'm sure I could have gone longer, but by the time I met JuleighAnn and got away from Evelyn, what was the point?"

Penn shook his head and looked out at the fields flying by, in transition from winter browns and tans to spring green. In time, the fields gave way to the city as they got on I-70 for the westward drive through Denver. Several minutes had passed without anything being said, and while Penn felt the familiar anxiety, Arden seemed perfectly comfortable with the silence.

"So you and JuleighAnn are pretty serious, huh?" Penn finally asked.

Arden smiled for a couple of seconds before making a response.

"Yeah, we are." He paused for a moment, then glanced at Penn. "She's great. You'll love her too." Then his voice became stern. "But don't love her too much. you'll have to get your own. She's mine."

"Don't worry," Penn replied with a smile. "I'll keep my hands off. I promise."

"What about you? Are you seeing anybody?"

"No, not since Shelley. I've been busy with work." He was silent for a moment, then looked at Arden. "Actually, that's just an excuse. I've told you on Facebook that I'm shy and introverted. I have been all my life. Growing up, I spent so much time alone in my room, I didn't realize I had a sister until I was in my teens."

"Really?" Arden asked.

"No, Arden, that's hyperbole."

"Smartass."

Arden moved to the right and exited I-70, getting on I-25 south. Penn could see the cluster of buildings ahead that made up downtown Denver.

"I don't know if all that time alone made me shy and introverted," he continued, "or if being shy and introverted is what led me to spend all that time alone. But I just freeze up and feel unable to converse."

"You're doing fine now," Arden countered.

"You're not a good-looking woman."

"You should see me in stiletto heels and my little black dress!"

"Oh my god! Thank you very much for planting that image in my brain," Penn replied with a shudder. After a few moments passed, he regained his composure. "But seriously, Arden, you and I have conversed online, so you're not a stranger to me anymore. I feel like I know you. And if nothing else, we have the common ground of being creatives. That makes it a little easier for me, too."

"Hmm," Arden mused.

"I usually think of something I should have said hours after the attempted conversation."

"Well, that happens to everybody."

"Yeah, well multiply that by most of the time, and that's where I am. Put me in a crowd of people and it goes off the chart."

"Damn, you're a mess."

"Thanks," Penn said, but he said it with a smile.

"Well, we're having a couple of friends over for a barbecue tomorrow afternoon," Arden said. He quickly tried to sound reassuring. "But only a couple. It'll be a small gathering."

"That's fine. It sounds like fun."

They were quiet for a while as they drove south past downtown, the early Saturday afternoon traffic fairly heavy but moving along at the speed limit. Then Arden exited again, heading west on what the signs called 6th Avenue, but Penn noticed it was still a freeway. And the farther west they went, the closer the foothills loomed.

All told, the drive from the airport took about forty minutes. By this time, they were in a nice suburban neighborhood, with well-kept twenty- and thirty-year-old houses and older trees. The lawns were neat and several of the houses had colorful flowers in carefully tended flower beds. The trees had a fuzzy green look about them, preparing to display their spring foliage.

They pulled into the driveway of a nice grey two-story house with a linden tree in front.

"Home sweet home," Arden said.

JuleighAnn hadn't had much time to read. After Arden left yesterday to pick up Penn at the airport, one of her hospital contacts had called with specific information about a patient she would be seeing on Monday. That call necessitated another call and a little research.

After that was all done, followed by a little last minute neatening up around the house, Arden was back and the afternoon was spent getting to know Penn.

She liked him. A very nice and good looking guy, though he was a little shy at first. But he seemed to hold his own with Arden, and with JuleighAnn, he opened up and seemed very natural and likable.

Now, on Sunday morning, she was awake before Arden and, in the early light filtering through the windows, she was attempting to read a little more of *Green Eyed Lady*.

> Augustine slipped his sword back into its sheath, as his adversary lay vanquished at his feet. The constable, Bubba, came to Gus' side and looked down at the man.
>
> "Poor dumb galoot," he said.

"Indeed," Gus agreed. "I hated to dispatch the fellow, but verily, the nave left me no choice."

"Hmm," Constable Bubba nodded.

"Did he have any family?" Gus asked.

"Aye, a sister."

"Girlfriend?"

"No, Gus, that'd be downright gross. She was just his sister."

JuleighAnn snorted, and Arden stirred next to her. He looked up at her through bleary eyes as she smiled at him.

"What?" he asked.

"You're such a dork." She placed the bookmark back in the book and put it aside.

"What do you mean, I'm a dork? I'm just trying to sleep here!"

"Shut up," JuleighAnn said, and she leaned toward him and kissed him.

"Madam," Arden replied, "I think it's only fair to warn you that love scenes you see in movies are only make-believe. Morning breath is a very real threat."

"I'll be careful," JuleighAnn said with a sigh, and she swung a leg over Arden. She sat up and straddled him.

"Uh," Arden said, pondering her new position, "hmm. Well I don't know what Mr. Arches wrote that got you in this particular mood, but I'm very grateful for him."

"It's not what he wrote, it's just who he is," JuleighAnn said as she began rocking back and forth.

"Okay, then I'm grateful for who he is," Arden replied, but a little more softly now, responding to her actions.

"Didn't I tell you to be quiet?"

"Yes, ma'am."

As JuleighAnn continued her rocking, she could already feel the terrain changing under her. Watching Arden's face, she saw the love so openly displayed in his eyes, and her body responded almost immediately. Feeling warm and wet, she quickly pulled off her Golden Retriever Rescue of the Rockies t-shirt, with the big GRRR across the front.

Arden smiled, clearly preferring this new view. As he softly stroked her thighs, JuleighAnn felt him tilting his hips to rise up to meet her. He slipped his hands up over her hips, caressing her sides, his hands finally coming to rest on her breasts. She always loved that, and as he gently squeezed her nipples, she caught her breath, closed her eyes and inclined her head back.

After only a minute or so, Arden could begin to feel her warm wetness seeping through his jockey shorts as she continued rubbing against him. Arden guided her off of him and onto her back beside him. He started to slip his shorts down, and JuleighAnn impatiently helped him pull them off.

Arden rolled onto his side now, and as he began nibbling JuleighAnn's neck and collarbone, his hand found the soft folds between her legs, already wet and welcoming. With his fingertip, he rubbed her clitoris, gently at first, but he increased the intensity as he took her nipple in his mouth.

JuleighAnn responded by pressing her head back into the pillow, her breathing altered to something more like panting now. Arden slipped his index finger inside her, still rubbing her clit with his thumb, and he gently bit her nipple.

As a guttural groan escaped her lips, JuleighAnn grabbed Arden's head with her left hand, pressing him harder against her breast. With her right hand, she reached down and found his erect cock, and she sensed his sharp intake of breath as she began rubbing her hand up and down the length of the shaft.

After only a minute or so of Arden's digital manipulations, JuleighAnn wanted him inside her. She tilted her body toward him, gently pulling him with her right hand. Arden responded instantly by climbing on top of her as JuleighAnn guided him in, and they both uttered an ecstatic "Oh!" as he slipped inside.

As he continued thrusting into her, Arden looked into JuleighAnn's eyes, gazing intently back at him as she usually did when they were making love. The eye contact, combined with the physical intimacy, only deepened their love and attachment to each other.

Arden could feel JuleighAnn's telltale writhing under him, and he sensed that she was ready. He began pumping harder and faster, and she responded with a gasp, hooking her legs around his.

As he felt his climax approaching, he held JuleighAnn tightly, and she wrapped her arms around him. She raised her hips into each thrust, willing him to cum.

When at last the floodgates were breached, Arden stopped moving for a moment, enjoying his rapturous throbbing inside JuleighAnn's body. JuleighAnn took that opportunity to grab both of his buttocks, pressing him as deeply as possible into her, and they both stopped breathing for a moment.

JuleighAnn felt the exquisitely warm shudder in her body as her own climax quickly followed Arden's. Arden felt that shudder too, and he resumed the movement, though a little slower now. Both breathing again, in synchronized breaths, they regained each others' gaze, staring deeply as Arden's movements slowed.

As their breathing approached normal respirations again, Arden kissed away the little tears that usually formed in the outside corners of JuleighAnn's eyes during their lovemaking. He caressed her cheek and kissed her lips, and they both uttered a simultaneous sigh.

Still inside her, they rolled onto their sides, gripping each other tightly, holding on to the closeness as long as possible.

Looking over JuleighAnn's shoulder toward the door, Arden said, "Oh, I'm sorry Penn, did we disturb you?"

JuleighAnn felt a moment of panic until she saw the grin on Arden's face.

"Asshole," she said.

I received kind of a strange call just before you came over," JuleighAnn said as she prepared a salad. Kenzie was there with her in the kitchen, her mane of red hair subdued into a ponytail. "Jim called me." JuleighAnn looked up at Kenzie to gauge her reaction.

"Jim?" Kenzie echoed. She felt a tightness in her chest that she hadn't felt in months since she left her abusive husband.

"Yeah. He found my number in an address book and thought I might know how to contact you. He wants you to call him."

"Shit," Kenzie said under her breath. JuleighAnn nodded. "What did you tell him?"

"I told him I'd pass the message along to you. I didn't promise him that you would call. That's entirely up to you." JuleighAnn scraped the green onions she had just chopped into the salad. "You're still officially married to him, aren't you?"

"Mm-hmm," Kenzie nodded, distracted. Then she looked up at JuleighAnn. "Do you think it's about divorce papers? Did he say why he wants me to call?"

"No, he didn't. But considering the marriage, you do still kind of have some unfinished business with him. Maybe now is a good time to take care of it, now that you have someone who really cares about you, and can support you through it."

Kenzie nodded again. She glanced out the window where the others were gathered on the deck. Arden was at the grill, talking to Penn, his friend from Boston. Valerie and Shannon were standing together, watching Hunter throw a ball for Molson, JuleighAnn's Golden Retriever, and when Kenzie saw Hunter, she perked up and her eyes shined. JuleighAnn, watching surreptitiously from where she was working, thought Kenzie actually stood up a little straighter when she saw Hunter.

"Yeah," Kenzie said, "I guess I should give him a call."

"How did you and Jim ever get together?" JuleighAnn asked. Kenzie turned to look back at her, seeming a little disoriented, as if she were waking up to real life from a dream.

"Oh, it was through his sister, Lainey. She and I were friends in high school. We were both into art, but she was really good. She's a sculptor. She makes beautiful wood carvings."

JuleighAnn nodded as she ground fresh pepper over the salad. She wanted to ask more, in the hopes that talking about it might help Kenzie build the strength she would need to call Jim, but she heard her name being called from the deck. She looked up and saw Arden motioning to them to come out.

"Looks like they're ready for us," JuleighAnn said.

"I'm going to go play with Molson," Shannon said to Valerie. She had wolfed down a little food and was anxious to get away from these people.

"Okay, honey," Valerie replied as Shannon went down the steps from the deck to the grass.

Shannon admitted to herself that these people were not so bad. But she still felt uncomfortable with them. They were nice, they welcomed her and all that, but she still felt like an outcast. Of course, that was kind of the point of the piercings and the makeup, to separate herself from people like this.

But people like this were not really that bad. They were not like her teachers or other authority figures she had encountered. It was a little confusing, and so she chose to ignore it. Which was easy to do as Molson came bounding toward her.

It was already forgotten as she bent over to pet him.

"The man was lying there with three GSWs to the chest," Hunter said, approaching the end of the story he was telling about his time as a cop in North Carolina. "And he looked up at me and asked, 'Is it bad?'"

"You're smiling," Kenzie said, "so I assume it wasn't as bad as it looked."

"Well, he spent a few hours in surgery, but yeah, he survived and was able to stand trial."

"GSWs?" Valerie asked."

"Gunshot wounds," Hunter said.

"Do cops really say that?" Arden asked. "I've heard that on crime shows, but I thought it was just TV terminology."

"Yeah, we really say that. Why?"

"I assume it's meant to be shorter, like a nickname or an abbreviation. But have you realized that the initials 'GSW,' at five syllables, actually take longer to say than the complete words, 'gunshot wound'?"

Hunter thought for a moment and smiled.

"What can I say? Cops love acronyms."

After that, the conversation morphed into a discussion about sports, which didn't interest Penn, or Valerie either, apparently. She got up and went to the railing around the deck to watch Shannon petting Molson down in the yard below.

Penn watched Valerie for a few moments, thinking back to a couple of hours before when he met her, and how he had done his typical freeze-up. He was struck by how attractive she was and he barely said 'hi.'

He thought he had covered it pretty well, though, as he met Shannon just after that. He thought she was kind of scary, with all the hardware and black makeup. But he wasn't attracted to her, and was able to utter a complete sentence to her.

Now, though, he was hoping he might be able to engage Valerie in an actual conversation. He put his plate down and got up from his chair. Taking a deep breath, he walked toward Valerie and leaned against the railing next to her. She looked up at him and smiled.

"Hi," she smiled. Her face was so pretty, but there was a sadness in her eyes that her smile didn't erase. "Nothing to add?" she asked, motioning with her head back toward the conversation behind them.

"Not usually," Penn said with a sigh.

"Not into sports?"

Penn decided that the best approach was to just be completely open and honest with her.

"Well no, not really. But the main thing is that I've just always been shy around people, especially around new people."

"Well, if it helps, I'm not new. I've been around for a few years." She smiled again, and Penn felt a certain comfort with her. "Penn," she said, "that's an unusual name."

"It's short for Pennington. Pennington Clark. I come from a very WASP-ish family who, despite their lower middle-class upbringing, loved the Anglo, upper crust sound of Pennington."

"I like it too." She took a sip of JuleighAnn's trademark white wine sangria.

"Thanks. You ought to meet my sister, Catherine of Aragon Clark."

Valerie quickly slapped her hand over her mouth to keep from spewing the sangria.

"Sorry," Penn said, embarrassed about his timing.

"No, it's okay," she said when she had regained her composure. "That was a good one." Penn felt his face flush a bit, as the embarrassment turned to pride. "So what do you do, Penn?"

"I'm an artist."

"Really? What's your medium?"

"I've done a little bit of everything, but nowadays I'm mainly a pixel pusher. I'm a freelance graphic designer and illustrator."

"Very interesting," she said. "You know, I think Arden does something like that, too."

"Yes, he does. We've traded a few stories and sobbed on each others' virtual shoulders until we were both able to get out on our own."

For the next hour or more, their conversation ranged from Valerie's history, to mountain living in Georgetown, to Boston, to Shannon. Penn was happy that he actually found Valerie easy to talk to.

Valerie glanced at Shannon, still tirelessly playing with Molson. Then, as if by a mutual agreement, Valerie and Penn both turned and went back to their seats, rejoining the others. Hunter was talking again, now about a current case.

"This kid knows computers like they were people. I mean he's kinda awkward with people, but he knows computers."

"And he found what you needed?" Arden asked.

"Yeah, he found it, and then some. I'm meeting with my FBI guy tomorrow. It's looking like he'll be able to reopen the case and we'll probably be able clear this kid's daddy's name."

"It's too bad his dad didn't live to see it," JuleighAnn said.

"I know. That's the one downside of the whole case," Hunter agreed. "But I'm glad we can at least do this much. And all because of this kid's ability to talk to computers."

"He talks to them, huh?" Arden smirked.

"Well, I don't know if he talks to them, but he can sure hear what they have to say."

Kenzie patted Hunter on the arm and he looked at her, and nodded as he got the reminder.

"Yeah," he said, "my little sweetiepie just reminded me that we need to go. I have an early appointment at the FBI and she starts her new job tomorrow."

"Oh, that's right," JuleighAnn said. "Congratulations. And good luck."

"Thanks," Kenzie replied.

"It's another gallery, isn't it?" Arden asked.

"That's right. My supervisor at my last gallery was kind of a jerk, so I went above his head and talked to the couple who own the gallery. They liked me," she smiled. "They didn't have an opening now, but they gave me a good recommendation. And it worked."

"That's great," Penn said, wanting to contribute to the conversation.

He looked over at Valerie, and he thought she seemed a little nervous, though he wasn't sure why. But she smiled at him as everyone stood to say goodbye to Hunter and Kenzie.

The drive home from Lakewood to southeast Denver only took about a half hour, but that was more than long enough for Kenzie to replay the conversation in JuleighAnn's kitchen.

And for that tight feeling in her chest to return.

She had known for some time that she would have to deal with Jim again. She couldn't remain married to him forever. But she had managed, for the last few months, to bury that knowledge under the happiness she felt now with Hunter.

She didn't think she was ready to deal with it just yet, though, and instead, prompted by JuleighAnn's question at the end of their conversation, she thought about Lainey, Jim's sister.

Their first meeting, in 1998, had been awkward, for Kenzie at least. She had a painting entered in her high school art fair, back when they still had art fairs.

She had been proud of her work. She was quite adept at creating realistic imagery, and her oil painting of the sky-line of downtown Denver was indeed realistic. She had captured the light and shadows, the reflections in the glass of the buildings, the clouds drifting by overhead, and the traffic on the streets below.

As reference, she had used a photograph she took a year or two earlier from the observation platform surrounding the gold dome of the capitol building. She had spent many long hours painstakingly duplicating the details of her photograph on canvas, over the course of nearly two months. Kenzie was understandably proud of her accomplishment.

Then along comes this brunette with a big nose who looked at the painting, long and thoughtfully, but screwed up her face in a frown. Kenzie had seen her around school but didn't have any classes with her. And okay, her nose wasn't *that* big, but there was just something about her that rubbed Kenzie the wrong way.

Like the way she was apparently critical of Kenzie's masterpiece.

"What?" Kenzie finally asked. The girl hadn't said anything, but Kenzie was, by now, thoroughly irritated.

The girl looked at her and actually smiled, unfazed by Kenzie's irritation.

"I'm sorry," she said. Her smile and her apology threw Kenzie off balance a bit, as she was completely prepared to hate her. "Your technique is flawless," the girl continued, looking back at the painting. "You have a real mastery of your brush. But I think this painting would have benefited from a little editing."

"Editing? What the hell do you know about art?" Kenzie asked.

"Well, I'm learning. I know a little about composition. I have a sculpture entered in the fair. I'm Lainey Stewart," and she put out her hand.

"Kenzie Collins." Kenzie reluctantly shook her hand.

Kenzie stood beside her and looked at the painting, trying to put aside her pride and see it with a critical eye.

"Okay, so what do you mean?"

"Well," Lainey pointed to the lower left of the painting, "you show part of Civic Center Park here, then some of the buildings of downtown, the City and County Building in the background. And it's a beautiful portrait of the city. But then," she pointed to the upper part of the painting, "here is a crane and other big equipment, and an ugly construction site. Big holes and piles of dirt. To me, it just kind of ruins the picture."

"But it's real. That's what was there."

"It didn't have to be for your painting."

"So you think I should have cropped it?"

"Crop it, or just paint something else there. Paint what they were building there as if it was finished."

"Hmm," Kenzie said, "I'm afraid my imagination isn't that good. I can paint what I see, but I have a hard time painting from imagination."

"Oh, I'll bet you could. Someone who can paint this beautifully must be able to see wonderful things!"

"You're making it very hard for me to hate you," Kenzie said.

"I don't want you to hate me," Lainey said, and she smiled at Kenzie again.

Kenzie looked back at the painting once more, looking at the big picture, rather than just the individual parts and her beautifully executed reproduction of them. She narrowed her eyes, looking through her eyelashes, allowing them to blur what she was looking at. She could see shapes only, a rough blocking in of the elements of the composition, unencumbered by the details.

And she could see it now. The construction site that she had spent so much time on was a scar on an otherwise beautiful urban portrait.

"You're right," she admitted. "I don't know how I didn't see it before."

"It's easy to do," Lainey said. "We get so caught up in details that we sometimes forget to put those details in the proper context."

"God, I'm embarrassed, now," Kenzie said, putting a hand up to her mouth. "I was so proud of this, and now it just looks like shit to me."

"No," Lainey protested, "it's not shit. It's beautiful work. But now, your next one will be even better!"

Her next one *was* better, but it took her even longer to do. She liked reproducing scenes around Denver, but she just couldn't get her imagination to kick in. So she relied on manually cropping her reference photos, which was okay in itself.

But then she started second-guessing her actual abilities. Why spend so much time and effort trying to realistically reproduce a photograph, when she could just blow up and crop the photograph?

While she was confident in her technical skill, she began questioning whether she had any real talent, or an artistic eye. Maybe she was just a good reproducer.

Lainey had encouraged her not to give up, but in the end, Kenzie's interest drifted to art history and aesthetics. Ultimately, instead of pursuing a creative life for herself, she took a job in a gallery, where she could promote the work of *real* artists.

Now, as they rounded a corner on their block and approached their house, she was brought back to the present. Her friendship with Lainey was good, but it reminded her again of Jim.

But Kenzie was starting a new job tomorrow, and she didn't want to be distracted by troubling thoughts about her ex. She was with the perfect man, now. Perfect for her, anyway. Nothing was going to spoil that.

Hunter glanced at her as he pulled up in their driveway, and she smiled at him.

H ow have you been doing, Shannon?" JuleighAnn asked. They were sitting in JuleighAnn's small but comfortable office off the living room. Shannon was absently tracing the pattern on the arm of her chair with her finger, apparently quite bored.

"Fine," Shannon replied, her voice expressing a complete disinterest in the proceedings.

JuleighAnn nodded, fully expecting this indifferent reaction.

"Valerie told me she's pretty worried about you. Why is that?"

"She didn't tell you?" Shannon said, hazarding a glance up at JuleighAnn. "I steal shit."

"Why do you do that?"

"It's fun."

JuleighAnn watched and waited. When a few seconds of silence had passed and Shannon looked up at her again, JuleighAnn raised her eyebrows in an expression that invited elaboration. Shannon huffed impatiently and rolled her eyes, thinking for a moment. After a couple of seconds, she resumed tracing the upholstery pattern.

"It makes me feel tingly. It's exciting. It's like getting high without the morning after."

"No morning after? Does that mean there aren't any consequences?" JuleighAnn asked, careful to keep blame and accusation out of her voice.

"I know there are consequences," Shannon said with another roll of her eyes. "But only if I get caught." Her smirk was all but imperceptible.

"Which you did."

"Which I did," Shannon echoed in a voice that indicated that she was already tired of the discussion.

"What about the consequences to the people you steal from? Do you ever think about them?"

Shannon was quiet for a moment, trying to suppress the return of her feelings of guilt.

This was going to be harder than she thought.

"How about I mix up some Manhattans?" Arden suggested.

"Sounds good to me," Penn replied, and Valerie nodded.

After a couple of minutes, Arden came back out and announced that he was out of sweet vermouth.

"There's a liquor store not far away," he said. "I'll be back in a few minutes."

"You don't need to make a special trip," Valerie said.

"Yeah, I can have something else," Penn agreed.

"Well, help yourself if you want," Arden said, "but my mouth's all set for a Manhattan. I won't be long."

Suddenly alone with Valerie, Penn felt the shyness settle over him once again. He began casting about for something to say and finding it harder to do.

"Would you like to walk down by the lake?" Valerie asked.

"Yes, that would be nice," Penn replied instantly, mentally showering her with blessings for saving him.

They walked down the steps from the deck, onto the grass, and toward the gate. Molson saw them coming and met them there, wagging his tail furiously, waiting for them to open it. Penn smiled guiltily at the forlorn look on the dog's face when he was left behind.

The sun had not set yet, though it was getting close to the mountains. The early evening air was a little cooler down by the water. As they walked closer to the water's edge, a group of ducks warily paddled farther out, keeping their eyes on the encroachers.

The shore was muddy, but covered with a mushy coating of last fall's leaves. There were even some thin patches of wet and crusty ice remaining in areas that were perpetually shaded by the trees.

"This is beautiful," Penn said, looking across the lake toward the groupings of cottonwoods on the opposite shore, with houses and townhomes peeking through.

"Yeah, it is. She got a great deal on this place."

"Have you known them long?"

"I've known JuleighAnn for years," Valerie replied. "I only met Arden about a year ago. And you've only known him through Facebook?"

"Right, for three or four years."

The ease Penn had felt talking to Valerie earlier was slipping away, now that they were alone. The conversation was beginning to bore him, so he was sure it must be doing the same to Valerie.

Suddenly, in another effort to be open and honest, he looked her directly in the eyes. His intensity seemed to startle her a little.

"I'm sorry," Penn said. "I'm afraid I don't make a very good first impression. I'm just so damn shy, I have a hard time knowing what to say."

Valerie smiled and shook her head.

"You don't have to worry about your first impression. You've already made it, and it was a good one."

"Really?" Penn was dubious.

"You made me laugh," Valerie said. "I didn't feel like laughing this afternoon, but you pulled it off."

"Thanks." Penn looked at Valerie for a moment, then turned back to the water. "But I'm just such a shitty conversationalist. I always have a hard time thinking of things to say."

"You did fine when we were talking on the deck."

"Yeah, well you did most of the talking. I mostly just answered your questions. I didn't initiate much."

"You know what I do if I can't think of something to say?" Valerie asked. Penn looked back at her and shook his head. "I don't say anything."

"You don't mind frequent deafening silences in a conversation?"

"Penn, I love silence. I live in a tiny town in the mountains. Other than the sound of the creek outside my back door, it's a quiet place. And I like it that way."

Penn looked at her for a moment, wondering if she was being truthful with him. She was so different from other women he had been attracted to. He always seemed to be drawn to exuberant, outgoing women, like Shelley.

"You really don't think I'm boring if I don't say anything?"

"Look, Penn, I don't need a steady stream of conversation. I don't know what you've been told in the past, but you're just fine the way you are. I like you."

Valerie had taken a half step toward him. In that slight movement, her foot slipped on a layer of muddy leaves, and she let out a surprised whoop. In the moment that Penn saw her foot slip out from under her, he grabbed for her, his left arm around her back, catching her right hand in his.

With that rapid movement, his own feet slipped too, but with his legs spread apart, he found some stability, and kept Valerie from going down.

"Whatever you think you lack in conversational skills," Valerie said a little breathlessly, "you certainly make up for in quick reflexes."

Penn smiled as he helped to steady her on her feet.

They were not quick to let go of each other's hands, though.

Shannon looked at Valerie as they drove back up into the mountains toward Georgetown. Shannon didn't know what was going on with her, but she was fine with how distracted Valerie was.

When her session with JuleighAnn was over, they had come out of her office and found Arden, his friend Penn, and Valerie in the family room, a small fire going in the gas fireplace. Valerie was sitting next to Penn in the love seat, and she was smiling.

Shannon realized that it had been quite a while since she had seen Valerie really smiling.

They had stayed and visited a while longer, or rather, the four older people had visited. Shannon didn't really participate.

Then, as they were leaving, she noticed that Valerie suddenly seemed almost sad. And her hand lingered in Penn's.

In the years that Shannon had lived with Valerie, she had witnessed countless men vying for her heart – or even for just a date. After her fucked up marriage, Valerie had become adept at rebuffing men.

Shannon didn't know a lot about Valerie's marriage to Bill Luboff. Just anecdotes that she had heard at different times, or occasionally overheard.

She knew that he had a violent temper and had hit her a few times, and that he had essentially raped her. That's not the way a lot of people viewed it. He was Valerie's husband, after all. But fucking her against her will, usually when he was drunk, as far as Shannon was concerned, that was rape regardless of whether they were married.

Oddly enough, that's not what caused Valerie to leave him. She had stuck with him through several years of his violence. It was only when she learned that he was cheating on her. That was the last straw.

Some of Shannon's earliest memories were of Valerie after she had moved in with her and her parents. Shannon was a toddler at the time. Though Shannon didn't understand Valerie's emotions and her occasional weeping, her three-year-old heart reached out to her, attempting to comfort her.

And Valerie responded. She and Shannon quickly developed a close bond.

As Shannon grew up, she gradually noticed that Valerie was not interested in dating. She had started meeting with JuleighAnn to try to come to terms with her view of men, and as Shannon still was sympathetic, Valerie had shared some of her problems with Shannon, as well as some of what was discussed in her sessions.

An unintended result was that it seemed to affect the way Shannon viewed men as well.

But now, seeing Valerie apparently allowing herself to be attracted to Penn, Shannon was surprised. Valerie had hardly said two words since they started driving, and they were almost to Georgetown. She was obviously lost in her own thoughts.

Shannon hadn't really had much contact with Penn that evening, but he seemed like a nice guy. And very good-looking. She thought he had kind of shied away from her when he met her, but she wasn't sure if she had just imagined it or not. Because then he smiled at her, and even said it was nice to meet her.

She supposed that if Valerie was going to start dating, she could certainly do a lot worse than Penn.

High praise, coming from Shannon.

Shannon put her head back and thought about her session with JuleighAnn. Despite the awkward start, it had actually turned out fairly well. JuleighAnn had a way of making you trust, and even like her. She cared about Shannon and about the trouble she had gotten into.

After Shannon admitted to the feelings of guilt about her stealing, JuleighAnn seemed to think there was still hope for her. Shannon wasn't so sure, but she liked the fact that JuleighAnn thought so.

They had talked a little about Shannon's earlier years with Valerie, and even about what she could remember about her parents. That was where the session had started to get uncomfortable again, though she wasn't sure why.

JuleighAnn suggested that it was likely grief concerning her parents' death. Something else that was touched on which Shannon found interesting was the possibility that her tendency to steal could be related to the loss of her parents. Since they were unjustly taken from her, it helped her to justify taking things from others.

Shannon wasn't sure she believed that, and JuleighAnn had been careful to not say that was definitely the case, but it was an interesting theory anyway. JuleighAnn hoped to pursue it further, and by the time the session was over, Shannon was actually okay with seeing her again.

Back in her room now, Shannon opened up the laptop. The stolen laptop, she thought, as the guilt resurfaced again. She checked her e-mail, then opened the browser and went to Facebook.

Numerous notifications indicated that something was very wrong. Kevin, her friend in Portland, was dead. A couple of mutual friends had shared news stories about the stabbing.

He had been taking the trash out and hadn't come back in. When his mother went to see what was taking so long, she found his body in the alley.

There had been no witnesses, but the police said it was apparently not a robbery. His wallet and his iPhone were still in his pockets. They were investigating to see if there was anyone who had a grudge against him, but so far, his mother was unable to help them.

"He was a sweet kid," she said. "Everyone loved him!"

Shannon didn't really know Kevin except online, but she felt chilled by the news. She remembered her last contact with him, when she had delivered a Facebook poke last night.

She felt the tears welling up in her eyes.

"You fucking twat," she said to herself. "You didn't even know him." She wiped the tears from her eyes and continued perusing her notifications, determined to not be affected by what happened to somebody she didn't even know in real life.

After a half hour, she felt better. She had responded to some friends' remarks, posted a couple of things herself, and returned a poke to Jenny, a friend in Aurora, near Denver International Airport. Jenny was one of the friends that Shannon had been with at the airport early yesterday morning.

Only *she* hadn't gotten caught.

The late hour, along with the emotions she had felt earlier about Kevin, combined to make Shannon suddenly feel exhausted.

She closed the computer and went to bed.

Valerie stirred and stretched. The early morning sunlight streaming almost horizontally through her window, combined with the murmur of Clear Creek down below, eased her into wakefulness. She loved her cottage on the creek. Waking up here was always pleasant.

But she woke this morning with a strange tangle of emotions. She remembered the evening before, the barbecue and the time afterwards, with a feeling of warm comfort. Yet she now felt a tight uneasiness.

The desire to distance herself from men, which had gradually developed since her disastrous marriage to Bill, was returning, and she was surprised that she had disregarded her instincts last night. But Penn had been so disarming. His shyness, coupled with his sense of humor, was endearing.

The fact that she had allowed herself to get as close as she did in so short a time, she recognized that it was a good sign. But at the same time, she trembled with the thought of repeating past mistakes.

Feeling uncomfortable, she turned onto her side, then realized that the discomfort was more psychological than physical. As she lay in her otherwise empty bed, the uneasiness she felt brought back the unpleasant memory of her last day with Bill.

That morning, years ago, Bill lay sprawled out naked next to her, his head half buried in the pillow, snoring loudly. She looked contemptuously at him, then glanced up at the clock.

6:15, she thought. *He'll be asleep for several more hours.* She fought her gag reflex as she smelled the morning-after bourbon breath spilling from his mouth. Turning over, she rolled out of bed and walked quietly into the bathroom.

"Calgon, take me away," she said aloud as the hot water washed over her in the shower, remembering the cheesy TV commercials for the bubble bath. Some poor little woman living the modern American dream was always completely overwhelmed with her hectic life. But then, she would get in the bathtub and suddenly, magically, be transported to a peaceful, relaxing place.

"God, if only that would work," Valerie thought. No matter how hot the water was, no matter how long the shower, no matter how hard she scrubbed, she still felt dirty afterwards.

She dried off, then wiped the condensation from the mirror and looked at herself. Her shoulder-length hair at that time was the color of straw, and of a similar texture. She used to be pretty. But now, the lines showing around her eyes and the corners of her mouth made her look much older than her twenty-six years.

Her eyes moved down to the reflection of her body. It wasn't a curvy, feminine figure any longer, just thin. It reminded her of an old dress on a wire hanger. A lot of straight lines and sharp points. A memory of the features remained, but they were no longer filled out to their full potential.

She scoffed at the thought. *What potential?*

Looking back at her face, the image became blurry as she felt tears welling up. She was surprised by that since she had stopped caring some time back. She dried her eyes and looked away.

She pulled on her 'uniform' of sweatshirt and sweatpants. Valerie had not noticed the progressive deterioration of her self-esteem, but she had gradually stopped wearing makeup a couple of years before. What was the point? She didn't go out much since her friends had drifted away. It was too difficult to cultivate friendships when she had to put all her attention and effort into holding her marriage together. But she didn't want to admit her inability in this area. She and Bill had not made love in years, but had sex fairly frequently, usually when he was drunk. Last night was no different.

She tried to force the memory from her mind.

She dragged her feet into the kitchen, but it took some effort for her to make coffee. It took effort to do anything anymore. As she poured the water in the coffee maker, she reluctantly analyzed her life. She had long ago trained herself to not think too much about it. That made it easier for her to cope. She sighed.

As the coffee brewed, she started cleaning up the kitchen from the night before. Dirty dishes were still in the sink and on the counter. Dinner hadn't turned out the way she had expected. But it wasn't the first time.

For a few years, Valerie made excuses for Bill. Her older brother Peter never liked him, though he was diplomatic about it. Peter, from the time he was young, had an uncanny ability to accurately size people up, and he had seen through Bill's politeness. There was something about him that was not right.

But Valerie refused to listen. They loved each other and nobody was going to come between them. It felt like such a romantic struggle, so 'Romeo and Juliet,' and she wouldn't give up. They were married six months after they met.

She noticed shortly after the wedding that Bill drank more than he should. She shrugged it off as just a difference in his upbringing. He had no family and his life had been hard.

Plus, their neighborhood in Highlands Ranch, south of Denver, was an expensive place to live, and Bill was unskilled. The jobs he was able to get didn't pay as much as he would have liked, which made for added stress. The bills piled up, the jobs came and went, and Bill hid behind his bourbon.

Valerie knew now not to bring up the subject of his drinking. She had learned early on how much it hurts to be hit with a man's fist.

The day before, when she heard the front door slam in the late afternoon, she was instantly on alert. She went to greet Bill, to assess the situation and determine what kind of support he needed.

"You're home early," she said, affecting a cheerful voice, and she immediately regretted the obvious remark. Bill was apparently irritated by it too.

"No shit," he snarled. "I got fired. That asshole Avery finally got his way."

Bill versus the world. Somebody was always against him.

"Oh honey, I'm sorry," Valerie said, trying to comfort him. She tried to rub his shoulders but he pushed her away.

"Is dinner ready?" he asked.

"Not yet," she replied meekly. "But I could hurry it along if you're hungry."

"I am," he said gruffly as he made his way to the liquor cabinet.

Valerie knew not to get in his way. She followed him into the kitchen and busied herself with the food that she had just recently started preparing. Bill poured his drink and left, and a few moments later, Valerie heard the TV in the living room.

She tried a couple of times to engage him in conversation during dinner, to find out what had happened this time at work, but Bill wasn't interested. The rest of the evening was quiet until Bill was ready to go to bed.

Now he wanted to be near her.

Hoping that he might have had enough to drink that he would just drift off to sleep, Valerie remained quiet and calm, helping him to bed, talking soothingly. But Bill was still alert enough to grab her and roughly pull her down beside him.

"You should probably start looking for another job tomorrow," she suggested. "Maybe you should just get some sleep." Again, she instantly knew it was the wrong thing to say. She had to be more careful.

"Maybe you should just get your skinny ass in bed," he slurred.

"Okay," she said quietly, knowing it was useless to fight him.

She started getting undressed, but was not moving fast enough for Bill. He was already naked – and erect, she noticed – and he began helping her get her underwear off. She felt herself shutting down as she often did.

There was no preamble. Bill pushed her down on the bed, spread her legs and entered her. He didn't bother to look at her or hold her. He kept his head up, looking at the wall, as he thrust into her. She was disgusted by the act but knew that she couldn't express this.

"Don't look at him," she told herself. "Just keep your eyes closed. Be patient. It'll be over soon."

And it was. A minute later, he was done. He pulled out of her, gasping from the exertion, and rolled over away from her. Within a few minutes, he was asleep. She rolled over into a fetal position and quietly cried.

The coffee maker finished brewing and pulled her back into her morning after. She poured a cup of coffee and padded barefoot through the house. Feeling an almost tangible pain in her chest, she looked at photographs of her family in happier times.

She knew that Peter had been right about Bill. Why hadn't she listened? Why did she have to be such a stupid kid?

Peter would occasionally hint that she should leave Bill. It always rang true with her, and she would catch herself almost daydreaming about doing that.

How can I leave Bill? she scoffed. She had married him when she was only nineteen. She never went to college. Never had a real job. She had no skills and very little work experience. *I'd never be able to support myself.*

Bill stubbornly held on to the archaic belief that a woman's place is in the home. And yet despite that, Valerie sometimes got the feeling that he resented her for not contributing financially.

Continuing through the house, she walked through a shaft of early morning sunlight and felt her eyes involuntarily squint. That action squeezed out the tears that had been resting on her eyelids and, as if it had primed the pump, a torrent followed. She sat down on the window seat and gave in to it, hard sobs that shook her whole body.

After a few minutes of this, she was left trembling but felt a little better. The intensity of her emotions on the heels of the morning's introspection and the memory of her brother's warnings, seemed to give her a feeling of strength. Wondering what she should do with it, she decided that it was time to get busy.

She again impatiently wiped tears from her face and re-traced her steps through the house, picking things up and putting them away. She left her empty coffee cup on the kitchen counter and went back into the bedroom, noting that Bill was still sleeping soundly. She walked around the bed, gathering up articles of clothing that had been shed the night before and followed the trail into the bathroom.

In the brighter light of the bathroom, she noticed a smear of something on Bill's shirt. It looked like makeup. Looking up into the mirror at her own unretouched face, she hesitantly sniffed the shirt and detected a trace of per-fume, realizing immediately that Bill had not come straight home yesterday.

That morning, she had quietly packed a couple of bags and moved in with Peter and Kristy before Bill even woke up.

Back in the present, lying in her bed in Georgetown, Valerie realized that she was once again in a fetal position. She rolled onto her back and stretched again, trying to rid her mind of the unwelcome memories.

She knew that Bill was only one man, certainly not rep-resentative of the entire gender. Valerie was a good look-ing woman, and men were interested. But Bill had messed her up.

In December, during the Georgetown Christmas Mar-ket, their annual holiday festival, she stopped to visit with Marshal Goldsmith and a couple of Colorado Rangers pa-trolling along 6th Street, the town's main business route.

One of the Rangers, Tom Blevins, had been interested in Valerie for a while. She had even agreed to dinner with him once, although she stopped short of calling it a date. And even though she admitted to herself that Tom was a nice guy, polite and a true gentleman, she avoided all follow-up attempts.

"Good morning, Valerie," he had said with a pleasant smile, tilting his head toward her in a way that made her think of men who tipped their hats to women a century before.

"Hi, Tom," she said, uncomfortably aware of his continued interest. She greeted the other two men as well. They were friendly and polite too, but it seemed like they both backed up slightly, as if allowing her and Tom a little symbolic privacy.

Then again, maybe it was just her imagination.

"Have you had breakfast yet?" Tom asked. "The Happy Cooker's sounding awfully good this morning." They were standing right in front of The Happy Cooker, one of the more popular restaurants in Georgetown, often with a line of customers waiting to be seated.

"I have," Valerie replied. "But thank you."

Tom put a hand gently on her shoulder and stepped away from his companions a few feet. When they had gained a little actual privacy, he spoke quietly.

"Valerie, I know you've been through some tough shit. I mean I don't know any details, and I'm not asking for any. But I like you a lot, and I'm here if you ever need someone to talk to."

"I know, Tom," she replied, her tone almost embarrassed. "I appreciate that, but I'm fine. Really." Tom's expression was subtle, but she caught it. The fleeting look of disbelief on his face. "I'm not really ready for a relationship just yet."

She tried not to think about the fact that, at the time, it had been over fourteen years since she had left Bill. That seemed like a long time, even to her. Tom nodded.

"Well," he said, "I'm here. If there's ever anything you need, you just call."

Valerie noticed a tone of finality in his voice, almost as if he had finally decided his efforts were hopeless.

"I know," she replied. "Thank you, Tom. I really need to go," she added hastily. She nodded a good-bye to the other two in the background, noticing the look of sympathy they cast toward their smitten friend.

Tom was just the latest in a string of men who had attempted closeness and been rebuffed. She was flattered by the attention and, as always, felt bad that she couldn't bring herself to open up to any of them.

She let out a sigh and rolled onto her side.

In the end, her inner demons won out again. Even before she had gotten out of bed, Penn texted her to ask her to dinner that night.

She declined.

Approximately four miles southeast of downtown Denver, there used to be a major blight on the land. A huge pit from which sand had been mined lay open and empty like a gaping wound.

As humans often do, the city of Denver thought that a giant hole in the ground would be a perfect place to dump their garbage. So in the 1940s, the former sand pit was turned into a landfill.

After it was filled with garbage, the first Cherry Creek Mall was built on top of it. Eventually it was torn down, to be replaced by the current mall, opened in 1990, and now anchored by such upscale stores as Nordstrom, Macy's and Neiman Marcus.

Just north of the mall, across First Avenue, is Cherry Creek North, sixteen city blocks filled with premium galleries, boutiques, restaurants and spas. Right in the middle of Cherry Creek North, behind floor-to-ceiling glass, was the Zephyr Fine Art Gallery.

The staff of Zephyr was friendly and personable, and they helped Kenzie feel comfortable and right-at-home in her new position. Since it was a busy gallery with people constantly coming in to look, and occasionally to buy, the staff alternated their lunch breaks. It was Kenzie's turn, and she was sitting on the patio at the Cherry Creek Grille, enjoying the spring sunshine.

Away from the distractions of her new job, her thoughts drifted back again to memories of her growing friendship with Lainey. Returning with those memories of Lainey were the thoughts that she would have to deal with Jim, but her first day on the job was not a good time for that.

She remembered the first time she visited Lainey's studio, a couple of days after the high school art fair where they had met. The studio was an old, freestanding shed behind her house that her father had cleaned up for her. A small window in each of the four walls provided lighting and ventilation.

Kenzie knocked on the open door, and Lainey looked up from the rough block of ash that she was just starting to chisel away at.

"Hey, you!" Lainey smiled. "Come in." She was wearing old ripped overalls a couple of sizes too big for her.

"Thanks for inviting me." Kenzie stepped cautiously into the shed, looking around at the work benches strewn with chisels, gouges, rasps and assorted other tools. There were also carvings in various stages of completion, including a wolf that was emerging from a chunk of cedar.

Seeing the detail and expression in the finished pieces, Kenzie was already feeling an artistic inferiority complex.

"Lainey," she said, "my god, these are incredible!"

"Oh, stop," Lainey said shyly. "But thanks."

Kenzie looked at Lainey, at the dirty overalls and the wood chips in her hair, the mallet and chisel in her hands.

"You look so butch!" she said with a grin.

"Yeah?" Lainey looked down at herself, then smiled at Kenzie and shrugged. "I guess it comes with the medium. Usually it's guys who like to wield knives and chisels and whittle on blocks of wood."

"Whittle?" Kenzie echoed, raising her eyebrows. She looked at the carvings again. "Lainey, these are so much more than just whittling! You've got a real gift!"

"Well, that's really nice of you to say!"

Kenzie looked at Lainey again, feeling herself drawn in by her sweetness and her perpetual good-natured smile.

"I mean it, Lainey. I've never seen such a combination of accuracy and beauty, even in artists who've been doing it for years!" Kenzie noticed that Lainey's face was flushed now, so she tried to ease up on the flattery. "I'm sorry. I didn't mean to embarrass you. I'm just impressed." She gently touched the face of the unfinished wolf sculpture. "How do you do it?"

"I just take a block of wood and cut away anything that doesn't look like a wolf."

Kenzie looked back at Lainey while her comment sunk in. Then she snorted as she laughed, and she slapped her hand over her mouth.

"You're a good audience," Lainey said. "Jimmy always thought that was a dumb joke."

"Jimmy?"

"My brother."

Kenzie became serious as the name clicked and she made the connection.

"Wait, Jim Stewart's your brother?"

"Yeah, except I usually call him Jimmy. He thinks it's stupid that he was named after an old actor."

Kenzie was familiar with Jim Stewart, though she didn't know him personally. Not quite the star of the football team, but he was a jock, good-looking and hunky. And they were seldom interested in nerdy, artsy girls. Kenzie had resigned herself to admiring him from afar.

"Uh oh," Lainey said, noticing the faraway look on Kenzie's face, "looks like Jimmy's got another fan."

"What?" Kenzie asked, as her attention was drawn back to Lainey. "Oh, sorry. No, I just didn't realize he was your brother."

"He'll be home in a little while," Lainey replied with a sly smile. "I'll introduce you."

Shannon was late to rise, having gone to sleep with a heavy heart. Though she had consciously tried to move beyond the news of her Facebook friend Kevin's murder, it was still weighing heavily on her mind. The fact that she didn't know him in real life had little effect.

To add to her mood, she had had the dream again. She remembered being in the back seat of the car, with her parents in the front. She didn't remember anything after that. All she knew was that the effect was always the same: she awoke with an overwhelming and chilling feeling of fear and sadness.

During the years since her parents' death, she experienced the dream, on average, once or twice a month. While she couldn't recall any frightening aspects of the dream, she knew that it had to do with the accident, having started shortly after that.

Over the years, having met with JuleighAnn and other therapists, some of Shannon's sessions with them had sunk in. In fact she had developed a mild fascination with the workings of the mind, to the point that she often developed diagnoses of herself and others.

In the case of the dream, she figured that it was about a traumatic event, the accident, which affected her deeply, and which her brain had to deal with and process. However, being such a horrific and painful event, her subconscious mind subsequently blocked it from her memory to protect her.

Since she didn't know of any way to remember or analyze the dream itself, she had developed the habit of instead focusing on something else, to get her mind off the negative feelings she woke up with. Not that that always worked. In fact, the dark posters on her walls and the music she listened to argued to the contrary.

But for now, she reached for her phone which was on the bedside table, its charger plugged into the wall. She often spent a few minutes in the morning, as she eased into wakefulness, perusing her Facebook notifications.

She hoped there wasn't anything more about Kevin.

Shannon always started at the bottom of the list of notifications, going from the oldest to the newest. The first notification she saw was of another poke, this time from Kaley, a friend in Colorado Springs. They were approaching a thousand pokes between them. She returned the poke without hesitation. Shannon worked her way up through the other notifications, which were primarily of silly memes shared by friends and a few miscellaneous, inconsequential status updates.

Then, toward the top, posted just an hour before, was a frantic update from Lissa, her other friend and partner in crime:

"OMG! I'm so fuckin sad. My friend Jenny Lynne is dead! Somebody stabbed her to death overnight. Nobody knows for sure what happened, but she's dead! Somebody fuckin killed her!"

Shannon caught her breath and sat up, rereading the message. The message blurred as her eyes filled with tears. She impatiently wiped her eyes and read it again. She couldn't believe that her friend was dead.

As she cried, she tried to continue reading. There were already several responses following Lissa's announcement, expressing sympathy and horror. One of the responses, though, was from Lissa herself, providing further information.

"It was apparently a sword. Fucker stabbed her through the heart, and it came out her back!"

"Oh my god, Jenny," Shannon cried, "oh my god." It continued as a sort of chant, as she rocked back and forth, the tears spilling down her face.

She hadn't realized her volume until Valerie opened the door and came in. She was wearing her bath robe, her hair was wet, and her face was worried.

"Shannon?" she said as she came toward the bed. "What is it, honey?"

Shannon looked up at her and the floodgates opened. Valerie sat beside her and held her, rocking her back and forth as she had been doing herself, and Shannon settled against Valerie's shoulder and sobbed.

"A sword?" Valerie asked in horror.

Shannon sipped her espresso and nodded as Valerie took her own cup as the Keurig finished its routine. She carried it around the counter and sat down on the stool next to Shannon. She looked at Shannon's face. It was pale, haggard, but a little less agitated.

"And you say you just had contact with her last night?"

"Well, not so much contact," Shannon replied. "I just poked her."

Valerie nodded. She spent plenty of time on Facebook herself, but she didn't see the point of 'poking' someone. It just always seemed pretty ridiculous to her.

"You know what's weird?" Shannon asked, crumpling up her forehead as she stared at the counter, thinking of something.

"What, honey?" Valerie responded, waiting. Shannon looked up at her.

"Another one of my Facebook friends was stabbed to death the night before."

"Oh my god!" Valerie said, putting her hand softly on Shannon's shoulder. "Was she near Jenny?"

"He," Shannon replied. "No, Kevin lives in Portland – lived," she corrected, "in Portland, Oregon."

"That *is* a weird coincidence," Valerie agreed.

"Shit! You know what's an even weirder coincidence?" Shannon asked as her eyes widened a bit. "I poked him the evening before, too. Just like Jenny."

Valerie waited, looking at her through narrowed eyes.

"Don't you see?" Shannon continued, "I caused this. I poked them both and they both died."

Valerie took a breath and turned her head slightly, struggling to not let her face show how stupid she thought that sounded.

She didn't succeed.

"Don't look at me like that, Val. I know it sounds crazy, but how else would you explain it?"

"A coincidence, honey. Tragic, yes, but a coincidence."

"No," Shannon shook her head. "Both of them being stabbed to death a thousand miles apart within the same day, that's a coincidence. But the fact that I poked both of them just hours before? Val, that's just too weird to be a coincidence. That's a connection."

"How? How does your poking them in Facebook have anything to do with what happens to them in real life? And why now, after all the pokes you've exchanged with people?"

"I don't know," Shannon replied, exasperated. "I don't have it all figured out, but two people I poked on Facebook in as many days were stabbed to death. Literally poked!" Shannon stopped as her eyes widened.

"What?" Valerie asked, almost afraid to hear what new crazy theory was going through Shannon's mind.

"I just remembered that I poked Kaley a little while ago."

"Kaley?"

"Another friend, in Colorado Springs." Shannon pulled her phone out of her pocket and opened up the Messenger app. Valerie shook her head as she watched her, hoping that maybe this was all just part of the mourning process.

Shannon turned her phone sideways so the keypad would be larger and she typed Kaley's name. When her friend's contact information showed up, Shannon began typing her message.

"Kaley, I don't know what the fuck's going on, but two people I poked in the last two days are dead now. Be careful. Don't be alone. Call the police!"

After she sent the message, she read it again, realizing it really did sound crazy. How could something that is done in Facebook translate to real life? She didn't discount the possibility that Valerie could be right, but she still felt it was too weird to be just a coincidence.

"I know it sounds crazy," she followed up. "I can't believe it myself. But look at Kevin Morgan's and Jenny Lynne's pages. I poked Kevin on Saturday and he was killed on Saturday night. Then I poked Jenny last night and she was killed overnight."

Didn't really help, she thought. It still sounded crazy. But at least she had warned her. Shannon hoped it really was all just an unbelievable coincidence. But in case it wasn't, she hoped that Kaley took the warning seriously.

Elliot Logan maneuvered his rusty twenty year old Ford Escort down Old South Gaylord Street, in southeast Denver. He felt completely out of his element in the trendy little shopping and eatery district, but it wasn't his idea.

He saw the café ahead, Riblets, and as he approached it, he scoffed at the cartoon frog mascot on the sign, made to look as if it were saying "riblets." Almost in front of the café was an empty diagonal parking space, and he pulled into it.

Between a BMW and a Lexus.

He got out and slammed the door, and he went to the door of the café. Once inside, he saw Hunter Sage at a table motioning him over.

Elliot walked through the little restaurant, looking at all the light-colored polished wood and modern art prints on the walls. The place was already full with the lunch crowd, and he noticed glances from some of the people as he walked past their tables. It might have been his imagination, but he knew he didn't fit in.

He felt underdressed in his dirty jeans and t-shirt.

"How ya doing, buddy?" Hunter asked with a smile as he got to the table.

"Good," Elliot replied simply as he settled into the chair. He saw that Hunter already had a beer in front of him.

"Good!" Hunter echoed, and he raised his hand, motioning to the waitress. She saw him and approached the table. She was pretty and looked about seven months pregnant, but she moved lightly, and she smiled when she reached the table.

"You beckoned?" she asked.

"Hi, PregNancy," Hunter said. The waitress smiled and glanced at Elliot out the corner of her eye, as if she were acknowledging Hunter's silly joke, and that she had already heard it a few times. Elliot noticed the name on her tag was Nancy. "My friend hasn't seen the menu yet, but I figure we could get him set up with a drink to start with."

"Sure thing," she said, and she turned her full attention to Elliot.

Elliot was taken by surprise, and looked at Hunter's glass.

"Uh, I'll just have a beer. Whatever he's having."

"You got it," Nancy said with another smile, and she walked away.

"Why don't you have a look at the menu," Hunter said, "see what you want to order, then we can talk business."

Elliot opened the menu and started looking down the page. The first page was sandwiches, and he noticed a tuna sandwich for $9.95, a BLT for $12.95, a barbecue beef sandwich for $16.95. He glanced up at Hunter.

"Anything you want," Hunter said. "My treat."

When Nancy returned with his beer, Hunter ordered the Southern BBQ Rib Plate, and Elliot settled on a cheeseburger and French fries. $14.95.

Elliot took a breath, sat back and sipped his beer. He looked mainly at Hunter, but his big blue eyes occasionally darted nervously from side to side. He hoped the beer would help him relax and feel more comfortable in this yuppie lunch joint.

"Well, son," Hunter said, "I won't keep you waiting in suspense any longer. I met my contact at the Bureau this morning and showed him what you found. He's agreed to reopen your dad's case and look into it."

"Yeah?" Elliot said, and really smiled for the first time.

"Yeah, he was impressed, not only with the fact that you found and cracked it, but also with the variety of the materials you found. All kinds of information about Ryan Flanagan's crime operation in Queens, plus the e-mail to that hacker. I mean it doesn't directly tell him to plant false information on your daddy's computer, so it's kind of circumstantial. But my friend said it'll definitely be enough to look into it."

"That's awesome, Hunter! Thanks, man."

"My pleasure, son."

"I just wish I could pay you more. I know you were doing me a favor when you took the case."

"Honestly, Elliot, it wasn't much of a case. I mean I didn't have to do much. I was more of a liaison than an investigator. You did most of the work."

"Well, I couldn't have done it without my dad's computer. You're the one that got it for me."

"About that," Hunter said, "the FBI wants the computer back. That's one of the conditions. Now that they know there was more information on the computer than they originally found, they want to have another look. After everything you've found, I imagine it's more face-saving than anything."

"That's fine, man. I got no need for it. I'm just glad my dad's going to be cleared."

Hunter nodded and took a drink of his beer. As he was setting the glass back down, his phone rang. He pulled it out of the case on his belt and looked at the display. There was no name and he didn't seem to recognize the number.

He looked at Elliot and mouthed "excuse me," and slid the receiver icon to the side to answer it.

"Hunter Sage." He listened for a few moments, then his face reflected recognition. "Oh, of course. Hi, Valerie." He listened for another minute or so, and then he looked up at Elliot. "I'm with him right now. You want to talk to him yourself, instead of me trying to translate?"

He nodded and pulled the phone away from his ear.

"It's an acquaintance of mine," he explained. "I was talking about this case, and I kinda bragged you up. She has a computer issue that's scaring her a little. You said you wished you could pay me more. Maybe you could do a favor for a friend?"

Elliot nodded nervously, and Hunter handed him the phone.

"Hello?"

"Hi, Elliot. My name is Valerie York. This may sound kind of silly, and it's probably not even possible. Now that I'm trying to put it into words, I'm almost embarrassed. But is there any way you can think of that an action that somebody takes in Facebook could be translated into something in real life?"

Elliot narrowed his eyes, a look of disbelief settling on his face.

"Uh, I'm not sure what you mean," he said slowly.

"Okay, in Facebook, my niece has poked two different people in the last couple of days, a thousand miles apart. Each of them, within a few hours of her poking them, was stabbed to death."

"You're right," Elliot said, wearing the expression he usually reserved for idiots and conservatives. "That *is* pretty silly." Then he looked up at Hunter, remembering that Valerie was a friend of his, and he tried to temper what he said. "No, Valerie, I can't think of any way that something like that could happen. It's probably just a really bizarre coincidence."

"Yeah," Valerie sighed. "That's pretty much what I figured. But Shannon, my niece, is really scared now, so I agreed to just check." She paused for a moment, but Elliot waited. "Anyway, thank you for your time. I'm sorry to have bothered you."

"No problem," Elliot said, and he handed the phone back to Hunter.

"That was fast," Hunter said.

"Yeah, it's pretty quick when the answer is a simple 'no.'"

"Well, I appreciate you listening to her," Hunter said as he slid the phone back in the case. "I don't know if I could have explained a Facebook problem."

"It's not a Facebook problem," Elliot replied. "It's just a silly, irrational – " Elliot stopped, remembering again that she was Hunter's friend. "It was nothing."

He was saved further embarrassment when PregNancy approached with their meals.

Lainey did indeed introduce Kenzie to her brother Jim. As it turned out, he had noticed her vivid red hair before that, but knew little more about her. Having just broken up with his blonde cheerleader girlfriend a week or two before, he was available and they hit it off instantly.

After a few months, though, Jim graduated and went to Colorado University in Boulder on a football scholarship, while Kenzie still had her senior year in high school ahead of her.

But even during her senior year, Kenzie had a reason to be at the Stewarts' house, because she and Lainey became fast friends.

"I feel like I'm constantly praising your work," Kenzie said one autumn afternoon.

"Yes, and it's *so* tiresome. I wish you'd stop." Lainey tried, but couldn't hold the serious expression.

"I know," Kenzie replied, "but I'm serious. You just continue to amaze me! You get such a beautiful, lifelike quality in your sculptures."

"Thank you. It really *is* nice to hear." Lainey was currently working on a carving of a basket containing a litter of kittens. She had already spent a great deal of time carving the woven wicker details on the outside and was now beginning to carve the bundle of kittens inside, standing up and looking out of the basket.

Kenzie looked at the rough portions of wood inside the basket.

"Even the unfinished part," she continued, "it's rough, but I can still see the shapes you've blocked out, and they're such perfect, appealing poses. But then, when you finish the piece, you soften the lines, and finesse the expressions of the animals, and you take my breath away!"

"Okay, stop," Lainey said, blushing but smiling, clearly pleased.

"Sorry."

Lainey purposely blew across the top of the carving, blowing wood shavings onto Kenzie's shirt.

"Bitch," Kenzie said with a smile, as she brushed the shavings off.

"Have you done any painting lately?" Lainey asked.

Kenzie suddenly looked embarrassed and lowered her eyes.

"No. I just can't seem to get it back."

"Oh, but honey, you're so good!" Lainey said pleadingly. "I want to see more from you!"

"Maybe someday. I'm really into the class I'm taking now, though, *The Modern Art Movement of the Twentieth Century*. It's fascinating!"

"Yeah, well I'm glad you like it, but I can see you're trying to change the subject."

Kenzie smiled, but didn't deny the accusation. She pivoted back and forth for a moment, hesitating, before she spoke.

"I just don't have anything to say right now about my own art," she said. "I do enjoy it, so I'm sure I'll get back into it again."

"Okay," Lainey said in a tone that indicated reluctant acceptance.

"I'm hungry," Kenzie said suddenly, seeing that she was now saved from the current conversation. "Let's go get something to eat.

Lainey tilted her head and looked at the unfinished piece in front of her. Then she nodded.

"Yeah, I guess this is as good a place to stop as any," she said. "Let me go change and brush some of the sawdust out of my hair."

They filed out of Lainey's studio and Kenzie waited while Lainey locked the door. Then they went in the back door and through the kitchen where Jill Stewart, Lainey's mother, was just starting to work on dinner.

"Oh, Mom," Lainey said, "we won't be here for dinner. We're going out."

"Leaves more for us," Jill said with a smile. Kenzie had determined that Lainey must have gotten her sweet, good-natured personality from her mother. Both of her parents were nice, but Jill was particularly pleasant and amiable.

"I'll be down in a minute," Lainey smiled at Kenzie, and Kenzie nodded a response. Lainey rushed out of the kitchen and clattered up the stairs.

"You going to Spanky's again?" Jill asked.

"Yeah, probably," Kenzie said. Spanky's Roadhouse, a popular sandwich restaurant on East Evans Avenue in south Denver, near the university, was one of their favorite places.

"Yeah, that's what I figured." Jill turned her attention back to kneading the added ingredients into two pounds of hamburger for a meatloaf. She glanced back up at Kenzie.

"You know, Kenzie, I think you look even better in the Rachel hairdo than that Jennifer Aniston girl does. It really suits you."

"Thank you," Kenzie smiled shyly, and she self-consciously put her hand up to her hair. "Have you heard anything from Jim?" she asked.

"Probably no more than you have. The Buffs are playing CSU this weekend in Fort Collins. He's in the starting lineup. He's pretty excited about that."

"Yeah, he told me that," Kenzie said. "Okay, I guess we're up to date."

Jill turned her face to Kenzie long enough to flash her a smile in response, then turned back to the counter.

They heard Lainey pounding around upstairs as she quickly changed, and Kenzie snorted as she and Jill exchanged another look.

"My little tomboy," Jill said shaking her head.

A couple of minutes later, they heard Lainey come pounding down the stairs. But then nearly half a minute passed, and Lainey didn't appear. Kenzie and Jill looked curiously at each other, and Kenzie went to check on her.

Lainey was lying in a heap at the foot of the stairs, stunned but coming around as Kenzie ran to her.

"Oh my god, Lainey!" Kenzie said. "Are you okay?"

Lainey pushed herself up and leaned back against the wall and smiled shakily at Kenzie.

"What? You're not accustomed to my delicate, ladylike carriage yet?" But then she winced as she apparently started feeling some pain. By this time, Jill had appeared, drying her hands on a kitchen towel.

"Honey, what happened?"

Lainey sighed and shook her head.

"I was running, like you're always telling me not to do," she said in a voice that said she didn't want to hear it again. Despite the attitude, there were tears in her eyes as she held her right leg. "I missed a step. Mom, I really did it this time. I think it might be broken."

I really like her," Penn said, "and I thought she liked me." Arden, JuleighAnn and Penn were taking a leisurely walk around the lake, enjoying the warm afternoon sunshine, although they were currently shaded by the cottonwoods lining the southern shore. For Molson, though, it was not so leisurely. Seeing a grouping of ducks near the shore ahead, he was straining against the leash in JuleighAnn's hand.

Penn was still a little distracted by his negative response from Valerie that morning.

"You really invited her on a date by a text message?" Arden asked.

"Yeah, well it was early. I wanted to do it before I lost my nerve, but I didn't want to wake her."

"She does like you, Penn," JuleighAnn insisted. "I could tell. Seriously, I've never seen her so comfortable with anyone, especially a man."

"But her response seemed so cold."

"Maybe that was just another example of the nature of texting," Arden said.

Penn nodded and sighed.

"Yeah, there is that." He paused for a moment, gathering his thoughts. "I don't know, she just seemed so abrupt in saying, 'No, I don't want to go to dinner with you!' It just really seemed like we hit it off last night."

"Did she really say she didn't want to go to dinner with you?" Arden asked.

"No, I was just being dramatic." Arden smiled and nodded. "But in response to my invitation, she said, 'No, sorry.' I don't know, it just seems to me that if you're going to decline an invitation to dinner, it deserves a little more elaboration than that."

"Be patient with her, Penn," JuleighAnn said. "She's been through a lot."

"I know," he replied, "we talked about her bad marriage and divorce. She's got scars, but so do I. And hers have had a lot more time to heal than mine have."

"Yeah, but hers go pretty deep. They were constantly reinforced by physical and emotional abuse. Then there was the death of her brother. And raising Shannon hasn't exactly been easy."

They rounded the eastern end of the lake and came out from under the shade of the trees. The afternoon sun warmed them, while it cast diamond glitter on the surface of the lake.

"You're right," Penn said. "Maybe it's just as well. I'm barely over Shelley. I'm not sure I want Valerie to be just a rebound."

"That's a good point," JuleighAnn said, and she smiled as she remembered a conversation she had with Kenzie the year before. "I'm reminded of something someone said to me once. She was in a bad marriage and was interested in someone else, and I warned her that he could turn out to be a rebound. She replied, 'I never understood what's wrong with that. What's the problem with finding some happiness after a bad relationship?'"

"Hmm," Penn nodded. "What did you tell her?"

"I said that there's nothing wrong with it, but that it's important to look for it with a clear head, and not a broken heart."

"You're a smart lady," Penn said.

"That's what she keeps telling me," Arden said.

"You know," Penn continued, "I don't think I have a broken heart, though. Shelley and I didn't really break up. We just kind of fizzled out months before. Still sad, but it's not as if I was dumped."

JuleighAnn recognized that Penn was just verbally processing his thoughts. She didn't give a response yet, but let him continue.

"And I wasn't really out looking for anything, either. Valerie just kind of fell into my arms. Literally."

"Wait, what?" Arden asked as he looked over at Penn.

Penn smiled at him.

"When you made your booze run last night, Valerie and I were down here looking at the lake. She slipped and I caught her." He sighed remembering the moment. "Damn! There was some definite electricity between us."

"Good thing you didn't get wet!"

JuleighAnn rolled her eyes and sighed. "Here, can you take Molson for a little while?" she asked, as she handed the leash to Arden. He took it from her, but he wasn't prepared for the pressure that the dog was applying to it. He stumbled a few steps ahead as Molson pulled toward another indignant grouping of ducks.

"Just give her a little time," JuleighAnn continued to Penn. "I'm sure she'll come around."

"I'm afraid a little is all I have. I'm only out here for a few days."

"Yeah, I know," JuleighAnn replied.

Seeing the sad expression on Penn's face, she got the feeling that he wasn't just unhappy about Valerie not going to dinner with him. He must have fallen hard and fast.

The lake is small, so it didn't take them long to walk the circumference of it. But Arden and Molson completed the circuit first, a few minutes ahead of JuleighAnn and Penn. They were waiting at the steps leading up to the gate into their back yard. Watching them approach, Molson was excited, panting and shifting back and forth, his tail wagging tirelessly. JuleighAnn smiled as she approached.

"You're acting like you haven't seen me in days!" she said, as she bent over to pet his head. The dog stopped panting, but leaned into her hand as she petted him.

Now that his pack was back together, Molson could once again turn his attention to other things around him, like the Canada geese a few yards beyond. As he started toward them, Arden, the leash still wrapped around his wrist, lost his balance in the mud on the shore. Just before he went down, Penn caught him.

"Déjà vu all over again," Penn commented.

"Yeah, you've got quick reflexes," JuleighAnn said.

"You sure do!" Arden agreed as he pulled Molson back. "Thanks." He leaned toward Penn and lowered his voice. "I felt that electricity you were talking about. Maybe you could take *me* out to dinner?"

"Maybe you should have let him go down," JuleighAnn said with a shake of her head.

Shannon came awake quickly and noticed that it was still dark. Looking at the clock, she saw that it was just after five o'clock in the morning. Normally, she would have just rolled over and gone back to sleep. But after the stress of the last couple of days, she felt like she wouldn't be sleeping any longer. At least not until she knew for sure that Kaley was safe.

She pulled her pillow up against the headboard, sat up a little and reached for her phone. It wasn't on her bedside table.

"Shit! Forgot to plug it in," she thought. The laptop, though, was still on the floor beside her bed where she had left it, so she reached for it.

The first thing she looked for, and happily found, was a response to her private message to Kaley, her friend in Colorado Springs.

"You dumb shit," Kaley wrote. "How is poking somebody on Facebook gonna kill them?"

Shannon already felt a little bit stupid, so the fact that Kaley followed up her message with a smiley helped ease the embarrassment a little. The time stamp, though, showed that the message was sent late last night. Shannon knew that a lot could have happened in the last several hours. She needed to make contact.

"I know it sounds crazy," she responded, "but I was worried. Losing two friends in two days sucks." Then, as an afterthought, she added, "Asshole," followed by her own smiley.

Kaley was a senior in high school so, this being a weekday, Shannon hoped to see a response soon. While she waited, she checked her notifications. They included a returned poke from Kaley.

Shannon ignored that one.

Before she had gotten through her notifications, though, the computer pinged with the notice of a private message. It was from Kaley.

"That IS pretty shitty. Sorry. But I'm still here, douche bag!"

Shannon put her head back against her headboard and sighed. She could feel waves of relief washing over her, and those waves left tears in her eyes. She looked back down at the computer to make a response.

"Good to know, bitch. I guess it really was just a crazy coincidence."

They spent a few minutes exchanging good-natured obscene insults until Kaley said she had to get ready for school.

"Okay," Shannon typed, smiling. "Glad you're still here, you dumb fuck."

Then she returned the poke.

In Colorado Springs, Albert Dyal put his coffee cup down on his desk next to his computer. He had already checked his e-mail while the coffee brewed, and now that it was ready, he wanted to check some notifications and follow up on some friends in Facebook.

After he settled in his chair, he took a sip of his coffee. Much better, he thought. He didn't think about the fact that he drank decaf. His doctor had said that caffeine was not helping his blood pressure, so he started drinking decaffeinated coffee instead. After getting past the initial headaches, he began to feel the same relief he had experienced with the regular coffee.

Must be psychological.

Albert had just started up Facebook when he heard an unusual sound from his computer. It was similar to the ping that sounded when somebody sent him a private message, but it was somewhat different. He was looking for some indication of what it meant when a window spontaneously opened up in front of his Facebook news feed. The heading on the window said: SP Assignment.

Subject: Kaley Angeli
Sex: Female
Age: 17
Physical Description:
Approximately 5'6", dark hair, brown eyes, olive skin, multiple piercings, tattoos on both arms, "tramp stamp" on lower back, Celtic

cross tattoo on back of neck. Often wears
dark makeup, dark clothing.
Address: 595 Pikes Peak Drive
          Colorado Springs, CO
Additional Information:
Attends General William J. Palmer High
School (senior).

Below this information was a collection of photographs,
apparently from her Facebook page. He thought she
looked kind of freaky. All the metal embedded in her face,
the stark black outlines around her eyes. Why do kids do
that shit to themselves?

But Albert was thrilled. This was his first assignment,
and he felt a nervous flutter of excitement.

Reading through the information again, he drank his
coffee quickly, anxious to get started. This Kaley girl was
not far away, so she should be easy to get to. Albert was
particularly happy that he was able to get to it right away.
Flexibility was one of the primary attributes required to be
a member, and as the owner of his own business, he had
the flexibility.

Albert printed the information and a couple of the photographs. Once he had hard copies, he shut down his computer. He took a deep breath, stood up and turned to the
wall behind him, opening the glass doors on his weapon
collection cabinet.

He knew just the one he wanted to use.

Kenzie was just about to walk out the door to go to work, when she spotted the box of Samoas on the kitchen counter. She hesitated just long enough for the desire to take root. She took a cookie out of the box and put it in her mouth, holding it with her teeth. She grabbed a couple more and left before she could decide she needed more.

The first one was gone before she was out of the garage. The sweet, crispy/chewy cookies were one of her weaknesses, and she realized as she started driving toward the gallery that they also reminded her of Lainey.

Jim had come home for Christmas in 1999, his first year of college. He had taken Kenzie out to lunch and then to a movie. They had been arguing on the way home, though, and when they got back to the Stewarts' house, Kenzie went out back to Lainey's studio.

It was cold outside, and getting dark as evening was setting in, but the studio was fairly warm, with two electric heaters placed in opposite corners of the little structure. Lainey was leaning on her crutches as she worked on her carving. She looked up and smiled as Kenzie came in.

"Hey, how was it?" she asked.

"It was good," Kenzie replied. "Tom Hanks is always good."

The Green Mile had been in the theaters for a couple of weeks, but neither Kenzie nor Jim had seen it yet. Having heard the positive reviews and word-of-mouth recommendations, that's the one they decided on.

"Yeah, I like him, too."

"There was an execution scene that was gross, though. Really creepy! But Jim thought it was 'awesome.' Jerk!"

"Typical guy," Lainey said with a shake of her head. "Here, this'll help," and she held out a box of Girl Scout cookies. "I always keep a stash out here. And I buy enough so that they last until the next time they come around."

Kenzie smiled and took a Samoa out of the box. As she took a bite, she looked at what Lainey was working on. She was finishing up the basket of kittens.

"I was hoping to be done with this one before now, but my stupid leg is slowing me down. Kind of hard to carve wood while balancing on one leg and crutches."

"Oh, but it's beautiful, Lainey. Those kittens are adorable!"

"Thanks," Lainey sighed.

"Are you okay?" Kenzie asked.

"Just tired. I never realized how much we rely on two legs. My body's just trying to compensate."

"When can you have this cast removed?"

"Another week!" Lainey said in a tone that indicated she couldn't wait. "I'm such a klutz! I couldn't just break my leg. I had to shatter both bones. When they had to piece them back together and put a couple of pins in them, that's what complicated the healing process."

"I'm sorry," Kenzie sympathized. "But another week? That's not so bad. You're almost there!"

"I know. I'm just impatient." Signs of Lainey's frustration vanished when her smile returned. She held out the box of cookies to Kenzie again, then took one for herself.

Lainey leaned back against her work bench and took a bite of her cookie. As she chewed it, she looked at Kenzie a little more closely.

"So," she said, narrowing her eyelids, "you and Jimmy seem to be getting pretty serious. Are you going to be my sister-in-law or what?"

Kenzie assumed a disgusted expression.

"Not if he keeps acting like an asshole, like he was about the movie! That guy's head was on fire, and Jim was carrying on about how cool that was."

Lainey's lip curled a little as she imagined the scene, but then Kenzie continued.

"But he *is* really sweet. He's *usually* very sensitive to my needs and behaves like a gentleman."

"Wait, this is Jimmy we're talking about?" Lainey asked.

Kenzie smiled and took another cookie.

"I wish you'd put these away," she said.

"Why? You're doing a pretty good job of it." Lainey pushed herself away from the work bench and steadied herself on her crutches. She closed up the box and slipped it behind a box of tools. "Why don't we go inside?" she said. "I think I'm done for the night. Could you turn off the heaters?"

She brushed herself off as Kenzie flicked the switches on the electric heaters and the orange filaments faded. The girls filed out the door, and as Lainey slipped her key in the lock, Kenzie waited behind her. She wasn't aware of Lainey losing her balance until they were both falling backwards, squealing all the way down. They ended up on the ground, Lainey's crutches splayed out on both sides of them.

Lainey laughed first, their three legs and a cast tangled up together. As she tried to wrestle the crutches back under control, Kenzie started laughing too. As they finally got their limbs separated and back into submission, Kenzie helped push Lainey back up.

"You really *are* a klutz!" she said.

Albert Dyal drove directly over to General William J. Palmer High School and scouted around. It was only six-thirty a.m. but there were already a few people around, likely faculty members. He knew he had plenty of time before Kaley Angeli started on her way. The only real problem was that he didn't know how she went to school – whether she rode the bus or walked, whether she got a ride with friends, or rode her bike.

Did high school students still ride their bikes to school?

But after driving around the school twice, he knew it would have to be done before she got there. The school was surrounded on all four sides by relatively busy streets, with no place to lie in wait.

He took Cheyenne Avenue northeast to Wahsatch Avenue and turned north, following what he determined to be the most direct route from her house. His eyes were constantly scanning back and forth, taking note of his surroundings with military precision.

Despite his familiar urban surroundings, the operation brought a nostalgic thrill to his heart. When he had enlisted in the Army a few years ago, his hope had been to eventually join the Special Forces, but it wasn't to be. He had made it through combat training, and even exchanged fire with Taliban forces in a gun battle in Afghanistan.

But that wasn't enough. Albert wanted to do more. He wanted to be instrumental in killing America's enemies. He wanted to be a hero.

And then those pussies in Navy Seal Team Six killed Osama bin Laden, one of the scenarios that Albert himself had fantasized about, and he was a little 'too vocal' about his ambitions. Red flags were raised and psychiatric evaluations followed.

He was sent back to the states for further evaluations before finally being discharged.

Obviously, the US Army wasn't interested in patriots!

Turns out the Marines weren't either. Or the Air Force. Or the Navy. After being turned away by every branch of the military, he finally gave up and went back home to Colorado Springs.

But now, engaging in recon maneuvers in his own town, he was elated. He lusted for his engagement with the enemy, but he forced himself to remain calm, so he wouldn't miss anything. He realized that it would be better to carry out his assignment closer to her home anyway. The farther she got from there, the more variables that could come into play, altering her route, and the greater Albert's chance that he could miss her.

He was in her neighborhood now, nice but simple little bungalows. And there is where he found the cover he needed. The subject's house was near the corner on a double lot. The southern portion of the property, on the cross street, was surrounded by a six-foot privacy fence.

Having driven around the block, Albert decided to park just south of the cross-street, facing north so he could see the sidewalk in front of the house, as well as the alley. And he quickly formulated a plan of action.

As he waited, fully exposed in the neighborhood, he was glad he had taken the time to put precautions into place. This *was* his first mission, but he had prepared in advance.

As soon as he had gotten his assignment that morning, he went out to his garage. He applied the magnetic racing stripes to the hood, roof and trunk of his car. Tested for adhesion up to 120 miles per hour, he had no fear that they would come off during a little drive through town. His white conservative-looking Chrysler now had wide red racing stripes. Amazing how sporty it looked now.

The next thing he had done was change the license plates. He hoped to carry out his assignment without attracting any attention, but just in case anybody did see him, he didn't want to take the chance of being tracked by his plates.

And Albert felt a little more protected behind the tinted glass, and disguised by the hat and sunglasses.

So at 7:15, knowing he likely had about a half hour to wait, he poured a cup of coffee from his thermos. He sat staring straight ahead, just past the fence where she would emerge if she came out the front door. It's possible she could leave by way of the back door and come out the alley, but he figured that wouldn't make sense. She would have to backtrack, to come back toward the street where Albert sat, to head toward the school.

Now that he was in place and had time to think, there was something that he couldn't quite reconcile. He thirsted for the fight, to protect America from its enemies. But was Kaley Angeli an enemy? A seventeen-year-old American girl was admittedly not the target he had in mind when he hoped to join the Special Forces.

She must be a threat in some way. Otherwise, why would she have been targeted? He exhaled heavily and took a sip of coffee. His combat training taught him not to think of his opponents as people, as individuals. They were enemies.

He would do what needs to be done.

He had other things to worry about, in relation to the girl's route to school. What if a friend picked her up? What if she rode the school bus and it picked her up right in front of her house? What if her mother drove her to school? What if she walked to school, but with friends? Would he be prepared to carry out his assignment in front of a witness?

Turned out he had nothing to worry about. At 7:43, the subject stepped out of the front yard and onto the sidewalk. Albert put his coffee cup in the cup holder and started his car. He knew it was her immediately, recognizing the tattoos, piercings and dark makeup. She was dressed all in black, even down to the clunky black motorcycle-style boots.

Albert put his car in gear and turned right, rounding the corner just as the girl was starting to cross the street. Hoping that the mental profile he had created was correct, he stopped, just a few feet from her. He kept the car in gear, his foot on the brake. The girl stopped abruptly and looked at him, wearing a cold, fuck-off expression.

Albert looked her up and down, blocking her way, and he put his window down. She was just a kid. Could he do it?

"What the fuck do you think you're doing, asshole?" she blustered. Albert smiled, knowing now that his 'mad at the world' profile of her was correct. And her belligerent attitude helped to strengthen his resolve. His smile just seemed to make the girl angrier though, and she stepped a little closer. "You want to move your fucking old man car out of the way?"

He didn't respond but continued smirking at her. One more step, and she leaned toward him, her black, vaguely greasy-looking hair swinging back and forth.

"You're blocking the road, you dumb shit," she said, her eyes wide, her mouth curled into a sneer. Her angry expression was proof that she was not at all expecting for him to reach out of his window with a bayonet and plunge it into her chest.

In an instant, Albert knew that he had hit the mark and he didn't need to stick around. Before she even hit the pavement, he moved his foot onto the accelerator and drove away. A glance in the rear view mirror showed a small, pitiful heap near the side of the road.

He picked up one of the napkins that he had saved from numerous fast-food places and wiped the bayonet clean. Tossing the napkin out the window, he drove toward home, smiling with the adrenaline rush.

Valerie was relaxing in the living room of her little Georgetown, Colorado cottage, a steaming cup of coffee within easy reach, her iPad propped in her lap. She was chatting with Pennington Clark in Facebook. She spent a fair amount of time on social media to feel connected to people, despite her solitary lifestyle. This morning, she had received a friend request from Penn.

After blowing off his text message and dinner invitation yesterday, she felt awkward, and hesitated for a few moments before she finally accepted the friend request. Now, though, after spending some virtual time with him, the awkwardness had fallen away and she was feeling as comfortable with him as she had a couple of days before at the barbecue.

Though she was still conscious of how her reaction yesterday might have been perceived.

"So, I imagine you're probably thinking I should schedule a few extra sessions with JuleighAnn, huh?" she typed.

She took a sip of coffee as she waited for Penn's response.

"Extra?" he replied. "Don't you need to have SOME sessions before you can have extra ones?"

She sighed, but smiled contritely.

"Okay, this is never going to work if you don't let me get away with anything."

"I'm sorry," Penn replied, "you're absolutely right. In fact, what I should have said is that you're fine just the way you are." As she read that, Valerie smiled. "Which you are, by the way," Penn added.

Valerie surprised herself when she saw that response and felt the tears come to her eyes.

"I'm definitely not," she typed, "but you just racked up a lot of points by saying it."

There was a shuffling sound as Shannon came down the stairs. Having satisfied herself earlier that Kaley was alright, she had been able to fall back to sleep for a few more hours.

"Good morning, honey," Valerie said, smiling at her over the open countertop that looked into the kitchen. Shannon grunted in response.

Her eyes at half-mast, Shannon stopped at the Keurig and selected an espresso K-cup. Valerie didn't like her coffee that strong and only got it for Shannon. After pushing the "Brew" button, Shannon saw her phone on the counter where she had left it.

She woke up the phone and spent a minute or so looking at a few random text messages and listening to a voicemail message. By the time the boiling water started being forced into the K-cup, she started the Facebook app.

Before the coffee maker was finished pouring the espresso into her cup, Shannon screamed as she dropped the phone on the counter. Backing up against the opposite wall, she wailed "No! No! No!"

Elliot sighed as he got out of Hunter's car, pulling his computer bag with him. He liked the cottage, and the setting, backed up right against the creek, the afternoon sun sparkling on the ripples. But he wasn't here for the scenery. He was here to tell this lady in person, instead of over the phone, that what she's afraid of is impossible.

Hunter walked around the car and they approached the little front porch together, walking past the numerous wind chimes made out of a variety of materials. The door opened before they knocked.

"Thank you so much for coming," said the pretty blonde woman. She looked like she was maybe forty, dressed in blue jeans and a sweat shirt. "Please come in."

She smiled, but her eyes looked sad. Elliot thought she had the face of the parent of a colicky baby, who was at the end of her rope.

"Valerie," Hunter said once they were inside the little house, "this is Elliot, the young man I was telling you about. If there's anything going wonky with your computer, Elliot's your man."

Elliot smiled shyly, but shook his head.

"Yeah, but like I told you yesterday on the phone, that really doesn't sound like a computer problem." Non-technical people irritated him. They always thought that computers were magical things, and if you just 'plug in' a few keystrokes of information, you can make them do anything.

"I understand," Valerie said. She spoke quietly, as if she didn't want to be overheard. "And I agree, it sounds pretty ridiculous. But we don't have any other ideas. I just want someone who knows about computers to talk to Shannon, my niece, and put her mind at rest."

The anxiety on her face and in her voice touched Elliot, as well as the fact that she was Hunter's friend. He did want to repay his debt to Hunter. He nodded his head.

Valerie led them through the kitchen and into the little living room. Elliot saw a black-haired girl sitting on the sofa, leaning forward with her elbows on her knees. She was rocking back and forth, her face in her hands.

"Shannon," Valerie said, "you remember Hunter? And this is Elliot." Shannon looked up, and Elliot nearly choked.

"Shit," he exclaimed under his breath, then he reached out and shook her hand, trying to ignore the 'weirdo alert' expression she was casting his way. "Hi, nice to meet you," he managed to say.

The chick was seriously hot! Her black hair and dark eyes gave her an exotic look. She had a few piercings, but not to the point of looking like a hardware store for the Walking Dead.

Elliot was glad he had finally replaced the paper clip in his ear with a new curved barbell. He wasn't sure about the t-shirt he was wearing, though, that said, "You turn my floppy into a hard drive!" At least not until he noticed Shannon look at it and smile slightly.

He saw the tears in her eyes and he felt protective of her, and he suddenly wanted to help her, to find what was wrong with her computer and fix it.

"Can I get you anything to drink?" Valerie asked.

Hunter saw their cups on the coffee table.

"Just some coffee if it's not too much trouble," he said.

"Plain coffee?" she asked.

"Yeah, just plain old black coffee," Hunter nodded with an amiable smile, as he pulled a pen and a notebook out of his pocket.

"We also have espresso," Shannon said softly, picking up her cup. Elliot looked from her dark eyes, down to her cup, and back up to her face.

"I'll have espresso," he said, and he thought he saw a hint of a smile again.

As Valerie prepared their coffees, Hunter and Elliot seated themselves around Shannon. Elliot gently put his bag down on the floor as Shannon began relating what had happened.

"Saturday night, I was on Facebook, and I poked a friend, Kevin Morgan in Portland, Oregon. We had exchanged over 700 pokes. Sunday evening, I found out he was dead. Somebody had stabbed him."

"Okay, see," Elliot said, "that's the thing. A computer program can't make somebody die of a stab wound." He instantly regretted his outspokenness, though, when he saw Shannon's eyes narrow at him.

"Yeah, I know that, genius. And at this point, I didn't think the poke had anything to do with his death. I didn't even remember it. But during that same session online, I poked another friend, Jenny Lynne. She was in Aurora, near the airport. She was stabbed to death overnight."

While she was talking, she fumbled nervously with her phone.

"Do you mind if I look at that?" Elliot asked. She readily handed it to him. He pulled his laptop out of his bag, along with a USB cord. As he plugged her phone into his computer, he looked up at her. "Keep going," he said.

"Then I found out yesterday morning, on Facebook, that Jenny was dead," Shannon said, and her voice broke. Elliot looked up from the phone as Shannon wiped away the tears. And he felt that same protective feeling.

"You knew her?" Hunter asked. "I mean in real life?"

"Yes," Shannon nodded. "We'd been friends for years."

"I'm sorry, hon," Hunter said. Elliot nodded his agreement.

"Yeah, that really sucks," he said, hoping it sounded sympathetic.

Valerie came in carrying two cups of coffee and set them down in front of the two visitors, as Shannon resumed her story.

"Anyway, at the same time, yesterday morning, I poked another friend, Kaley, down in Colorado Springs."

"And she was killed too?" Hunter asked.

"Well, not right away," Shannon replied, sounding confused. "I realized that I had poked Kevin and Jenny just

144

before they were killed, and I was scared for Kaley. I sent her a private message, warning her about the other two, and told her to be careful, and even to call the police. I was panicking. But last night, she replied to my message and told me I was being a fucking idiot. I got that message early this morning, and even had a short conversation with her until she had to get ready for school. By that time, I *felt* like a fucking idiot, and I poked her back.

"I went back to sleep for a while. When I got up and came downstairs, I was checking my phone, and I saw that she had been stabbed to death on her way to school."

Shannon snatched a tissue out of the box next to her and wiped her eyes. Elliot tried to stay focused on his diagnostic software, but he found his eyes, many times, drawn back to Shannon's face.

L ainey was sitting up in her hospital bed. After having been subjected to a multitude of tests, over the past several days, during which she had been poked and prodded countless times, she was tired. Her dark hair hung flat and lifeless on both sides of her face, and accented the similar color of the circles under her eyes.

Despite the way she felt, though, she was still, remarkably, wearing a smile.

"You know," Kenzie said, holding Lainey's hand, "it drives me crazy that you could be going through all this, and you still look so happy."

"Yeah, isn't she maddening?" Jim replied from the other side of the bed. It was late summer, 2001, and he was about to start his third year at CU Boulder, while Kenzie was preparing to begin her second year at Arapahoe Community College. Though she was still a little unsure of her major, her curriculum included several hands-on art courses, as well as art appreciation and art history classes.

Lainey's parents were in the room as well, seated near the opposite wall, but they were quiet. Their faces looked haggard, etched with concern for their daughter.

"Well," Lainey replied, "they say that smiling is good for you. It releases endorphins that help you feel better, and even has pain-relief qualities. So besides being a result of *being* happy, it can actually help to *make* you happy."

"Thank you, Dr. Lainey," Jim said.

"I just figure what good is frowning and being unhappy going to do?" Lainey continued undeterred. "It'll just make me and everybody around me feel worse. If whatever is happening can be changed, the doctors will find it. And if it can't, I might as well try to make the best of it."

Kenzie noticed a couple of times when Lainey had a little trouble forming the word she needed. That, along with balance issues – her klutziness – were among the main things that made them seek out the tests.

As if on cue, the door opened and Dr. Finney came in. A middle-aged man with no hair except for a silvery fringe around the back, he had a kindly face and a manner reminiscent of family doctors from several decades before.

"How's my little Lainey doing today?" he asked.

"You tell me, doc," Lainey replied. As he approached the bed, her parents rose and gathered around as well.

"Well," Dr. Finney said, "we do seem to have zeroed in on it." In one quick motion, he looked at the others around the bed, including Kenzie, then looked questioningly at Lainey.

"It's okay," she responded, "they're all family."

"Well," the doctor said, his face taking on a more serious demeanor, "the symptoms you've presented, frankly, pointed to a number of different possibilities. Often when that's the case, a diagnosis depends partly on eliminating some possibilities and examining what's left.

"We've eliminated several of them over the course of these tests. Follow-up tests, including, most recently, the MRI and the lumbar puncture, have directed us to a positive diagnosis.

"I'm afraid you have multiple sclerosis."

Kenzie glanced at Lainey who, while still trying to hold the smile, had tears in her eyes.

"I'm sure you've heard of that," the doctor continued softly. "What it is, exactly, is an inflammation due to lesions in the brain or on the spinal cord. Your nerve cells have an insulation layer, a cover that protects them. With multiple sclerosis, that insulation layer is damaged and can disrupt communication within your nervous system.

"It's kind of like the plastic coating on an electrical cord on a lamp. If the insulation gets damaged and exposes the wires, and the wires touch something metal, it can cause a short circuit, preventing electricity from reaching the lamp.

"Now obviously, that's a very simplified explanation. The human nervous system is much more complex, and a lot more factors come into play. But very basically, that's what's happening. The exposed nerve cells are kind of shorting out and preventing commands from traveling properly between your brain and your extremities."

"That's why I've become so clumsy," Lainey interjected.

"Multiple sclerosis does affect motor skills," the doctor nodded, "speech processes, things which we take for granted and often do without even thinking about them."

"What about a cure, doctor?" Mr. Stewart asked.

"Well, there are a number of treatment methods to help manage the symptoms. These treatments are designed, mainly, to try to improve function after an attack and, hopefully, prevent further attacks. As with most drugs, there are often adverse side-effects, but the drugs do have some effectiveness.

"In fact," he paused as he pulled a couple of colorful brochures out of the pocket of his white coat, "I can leave some information with you about a few possible treatment protocols." He paused and drew in a long breath. "But at present, I'm afraid there is no cure."

"She's going to have this for the rest of her life?" Jim asked, almost angrily. Kenzie felt her heart clench into a tight fist in her chest.

"I'm afraid so."

"Doctor?" Lainey asked softly. Everyone looked at her. "It's terminal, isn't it?"

As if in a grim tennis match, all heads turned back toward Dr. Finney. His head was bowed a little, as he looked at Lainey, then at the others in attendance.

"You may have many years of life ahead of you," he said, directing his attention back to Lainey. "I'm afraid there's no way to predict life expectancy at this stage."

Lainey raised her eyebrows as she continued to look at Dr. Finney. He seemed almost embarrassed when he finally continued.

"From this point, you *may* have as much as thirty years, but there's just no way to know for sure." He gingerly placed the brochures on the bed beside Lainey. "I'm very sorry."

Lainey smiled at the doctor as a tear slipped down her cheek, blazing a trail for the others to follow.

"Thank you, Dr. Finney," she said.

After Shannon related what had happened to her dead Facebook friends, she took a break to dab at her eyes and sip her espresso. Hunter reviewed the notes he had jotted down in his little notebook.

"Did Kevin, Jenny and Kaley know each other?" he asked.

"Not that I know of. I mean they sometimes responded to things I posted. They might have been Facebook friends, but I don't think they had ever met."

"Kaley was in school. How old was she?"

"Seventeen. Jenny was my age, eighteen."

"And Kevin?"

"I'm not sure. Somewhere in his twenties."

"What are you thinking?" Valerie asked Hunter.

"I don't know. Nothing, really. Three people with no tangible connection to each other. Separated, in Kevin's case, by over a thousand miles. I can't think of anything that could tie these murders together."

"Except me poking them," Shannon said. Elliot glanced up from his diagnostic software, but decided not to say anything.

"You said you poked Kaley twice," Hunter said. "The first time, you suspected something, and you warned her, but nothing happened."

"Right."

"Is there anything at all that was different about that time? Anything you can think of?"

"No, I don't think so."

"And it wasn't until after you poked her a second time that she was killed."

Shannon nodded, but Hunter recognized the look on her face, as if she was concentrating. He waited quietly as she drank the last of her espresso and sat back, thinking. There had to be something that she had missed. Some variable that she hadn't mentioned.

And then she remembered. The laptop.

And the moment she remembered it, she knew she was going to be in deeper trouble.

"What is it?" Valerie asked, seeing that recognition on Shannon's face.

Shannon looked at her but said nothing. She realized, though, that her breathing had speeded up.

"Shannon?" Valerie insisted.

"It's the laptop," Shannon finally said.

"What laptop?"

Shannon got up and headed toward the stairs. Valerie glanced at Hunter, then got up and followed her. She caught up to her in Shannon's room. Shannon was pulling the laptop out from under her bed.

"When did you get a laptop?" Valerie asked.

Shannon closed her eyes and paused, trying to think of a plan of action. She was already in deep shit. Might as well tell the truth.

"I stole it," she finally said, as she opened her eyes and looked at Valerie.

Valerie stammered a moment, then, unable to think of what to say, stopped trying. She just looked at Shannon. The disappointment displayed on her face was particularly effective, in that it hurt Shannon more than if Valerie had scolded her.

"Val, I know it's wrong," Shannon said, her voice taking on a pleading quality. "We've already talked about it. This is something I stole before."

"So it's alright, then?"

"No, I'm not saying it's alright. Just that it's history. I haven't stolen anything since this weekend. Since we talked about it."

Valerie sighed. She shook her head and stepped aside, allowing Shannon through the door. But she stopped her as she passed.

"This isn't over, young lady," she said. "We'll be talking about this some more. But for now, let's just get this situation taken care of."

Shannon's first reaction was annoyance, but she knew that she had no right to be annoyed. Because Valerie was right. It was time to face the guilt she had been feeling. She nodded and they went back downstairs.

Shannon settled back into her spot on the sofa and then just sat there for a while, silently looking at the laptop.

They say 'confession's good for the soul,' she thought. In a way, she already felt a little better now that Valerie knew.

"Alright, here's the thing," she finally said. "I stole this computer. I've done some shit that I'm not proud of, and I used to be really good at stealing."

Okay, the last time was only three and a half days ago, hardly time to prove that she had turned over a new leaf. But still, 'used to be' *did* sound better.

Elliot and Hunter exchanged glances, then looked back at Shannon, waiting for her to continue.

"The first time I used this was Saturday, after I cracked the password." Elliot perked up just a bit at that.

"How did you crack the password?" he asked.

"I have a program called gRam Cracker. It found the password pretty quickly."

"Okay," Hunter said, "let's try to stay on point, here."

"Right," Shannon said. She took a deep breath and continued. "I was messing around with it, seeing what was on it, and I found that the Chrome browser opened up with Facebook as the home page. It was for the previous owner of the computer, Don something."

"He's the *current* owner!" Valerie said vehemently. "We'll have to get it back to him."

"Okay, Val!" Shannon said with an irritated edge. She sighed and forced herself to calm down. "Anyway, that was when I poked Kevin. I didn't get on this computer again until Sunday evening, after the barbecue. That's when I found out that Kevin was dead, and also when I poked Jenny."

"Also on that computer?" Hunter asked.

"Yes." Shannon was staring at the coffee table, remembering her actions, as if they were projected there. "But yesterday morning, when I woke up, I reached for my phone, which was plugged in next to my bed. That was when I poked Kaley the first time. That was also when I learned that Jenny was dead."

"You're sure you poked Kaley on your phone?" Hunter asked. "Not the computer?"

"Yes."

"So throwing the laptop into the mix could kind of explain why it started suddenly, after over seven hundred harmless pokes," Hunter mused. Then he turned to Elliot. "And it might explain why you haven't found anything on her phone, yet."

"Well, no, it really doesn't, Hunter," Elliot countered. "It doesn't even begin to explain at all how somebody goes from being poked on Facebook to being stabbed to death in real life."

"Well no, you're right, it doesn't explain that. But it does give us a better idea where to focus our attention."

Elliot glared at Hunter for a moment, then sighed, remembering how much Hunter had helped him with the FBI in relation to Elliot's father. He shut down the diagnostic software on his computer and unplugged Shannon's phone.

Handing it back to her, he took the laptop from her and began connecting it to his computer, retracing the same steps he had just taken with her phone.

As Elliot worked quietly and Hunter continued reviewing his notes, they were unaware of the tension that was brewing and palpable between Valerie and Shannon. Shannon sat on the sofa staring down at her lap, only glancing at Valerie occasionally.

After a few minutes passed, Elliot spoke up.

"Well, I can't find anything wrong with this computer. No viruses, no malware. There's a little fragmentation, but not enough to really affect the speed or performance to any noticeable degree."

"I don't think we care about the speed or performance of the computer," Hunter said. "What about what we were talking about?"

"I'm afraid that's something that's out of the scope of my diagnostic software, because it's not something that's possible. This is just a really huge fucking waste of time."

Elliot's tone of voice told just how irritated he was about the whole thing, but again, when he looked up at Hunter, he felt bad about his outburst. "Look, Hunter, I really appreciate what you've done, interceding with the FBI for me. And I'd love to help you out with this. But this isn't a computer issue.

"I can't explain how those people were killed shortly after Shannon poked them." He glanced at Shannon and his eyes lingered on her face as if magnetically attracted, and his tone softened a bit. "But I'm inclined to write it off as just a really weird coincidence."

"I understand, son," Hunter said patiently. "But we're kind of at a loss here. We don't know where to go, either.

We're open to other ideas, but at the moment, they ain't presenting themselves.

"And the only thing we can think of for now is the computer. And you're the only computer expert we know. If you end up eliminating it as the culprit for absolute certain, then so be it. But I'd really just appreciate anything you can think of."

Elliot stared at Hunter for a few moments, followed by another look at Shannon. The look on her face – well, he wasn't sure if that look was because of her being in trouble with her aunt, or because she was scared and sad about her friends being killed. But that look melted his heart.

"Okay," he said with a nod. He started copying folders from the stolen laptop to his own computer. He located the Google folder and, knowing that the Chrome browser software was inside, dragged it to his computer as well. "I'm copying the software to my computer. I'll take it home and have a look at the code and see if anything looks wonky, as you called it," and he looked at Hunter. "But I really don't want you guys to get your hopes up. I'll be honest with you, I'm doing this for Hunter, but I still think it's a major waste of time."

"Thank you," Shannon said in a tone that made Elliot feel as if he was rescuing her from the clutches of an evil wizard instead of just looking at her computer. He held her gaze for a few moments.

"I want you to know, though, that we're talking about millions of lines of code. It's going to take time to go through it."

"I understand," Shannon replied, and she treated him to a smile.

On a whim, he opened up Chrome and, seeing that Shannon had kept Facebook as her home page, he searched for his own name and sent a friend request. He pulled out his phone and accepted it.

"We're friends on Facebook, now," he said to Shannon. "*If* I find anything, I'll PM you."

"PM?" Hunter asked.

"Private message. But again, I really don't expect to find anything."

Jim Stewart loved the beginning of an offensive play. Any offensive play. He felt godlike. Yes, he depended on the other players to do their part – and they had damn well better – but he was the one who called the shots. Well, him and the coach.

He also loved home games. Not just because of the home field advantage, though there was a lot to be said about that. Folsom Field stood at more than a mile above sea level, and the elevation was not always that easy for visiting teams to acclimate to.

But he loved home games because Kenzie would often come and watch. He knew she was up in the stands now, along with his family, including Lainey who had ventured out in her wheelchair.

Football movies that showed the players getting into their positions in slow-motion, the sounds muffled, the crowd an indistinct roar – that was almost the way it seemed to him. Like it was not quite real-time.

He felt the cool October air chilling the sweat on his arms as they broke huddle and approached the line of scrimmage. He took his position behind the center, looking both directions at the lines of gold helmets, the CU Buffalo emblem galloping on the sides. He dug his cleats into the grass, getting a firm stance.

Ahead of them, taking a defensive line, the Wildcats, wearing their bright red helmets, were getting into their crouch. As Jim called out the cadence, it still seemed slow-motion to him, yet in his mind, both the call and the play were as clear as could be.

The ball was snapped into his hands and he backed up a few steps, hearing the violent clash of helmets and pads in front of him. He waited, watching his wide receiver trying to get into position downfield.

But he wasn't clear. Two of Arizona's players were shadowing him. Jim watched impatiently as the Wildcat defensive line pushed closer to him. He took a few steps to the left, hoping to accelerate an opening to the receiver.

But it wasn't happening.

It was up to him!

As the tangle of Wildcats and Buffaloes were right at his feet, he tucked the ball up tight against him and jumped over an unidentified arm, weaving between the combatants who were still standing.

His legs pumping like pistons, Jim crossed the fifty yard line, then the forty. He was huffing, breathing in time with his stride, and again, it seemed to him like slow motion. He glanced behind him over his right shoulder and saw that he was in the clear. Even the closest Wildcats were several paces behind him.

He had this!

He crossed the thirty yard line, the twenty. Then, something on his left captured his attention – a step, a breath? He looked to his left and saw a Wildcat safety, not a big guy, but wiry and fast.

Where the hell did he come from?

Jim moved toward the right, approaching the goal on a more lateral line, but doing so allowed the defensive end for Arizona, behind him on the right, to close the gap a bit.

The defensive end dove for him, but missed, falling at his feet. Right at the ten yard line, Jim was leaping over him as the safety launched himself and took him down. Jim's foot lodged in the defensive end's armpit as the safety landed on top of him. Jim felt his knee pop as he went down.

The ball was down at the eight yard line, and a time out was called while Jim was briefly examined, then carried off the field. The Buffs claimed those eight yards, and eventually won the game, but without Jim at the helm.

Jim swam up through a post-surgical fog. He dragged his eyelids open and saw a blaze of red on his left. He felt a hand in his and he squeezed it a little, and the red blaze moved as Kenzie looked up at him.

"Hey, you," she said softly. "How are you feeling?"

He tried to focus on her face, with only partial success.

"I don't know," he mumbled. His knee felt numb, but he could tell that his leg was immobilized. He lifted his head a little and looked around the room. Aside from the two of them, the room was empty.

"Your family's here," Kenzie said. "They just went to the cafeteria to get something to eat."

At that moment, Jim saw the door being pushed open, and he pulled himself up in the bed a little, and seeing his effort, Kenzie pushed the button to elevate the head of the bed. Jim expected to see his family. Instead, a stranger walked in.

"I'm sorry," the man said just a shade above a whisper. "I don't mean to interrupt. Are you Jim Stewart?"

Jim nodded weakly. The effort of pulling himself up made his head spin a little. The man approached the bed with his hand outstretched.

"My name is Bobby Jaworski. I'm a scout for the New England Patriots." Suddenly, Jim felt wide awake. He reached out and shook Bobby's hand.

"Very nice to meet you, sir," Jim said.

"The pleasure's all mine, son. You played a hell of a game!"

"Thank you. I haven't heard how it turned out."

"The Buffs won," Kenzie said with a smile.

Jim smiled, and Jaworski turned his attention to Kenzie. "And you are?"

"Kenzie Collins," she replied, shaking his offered hand.

"Nice to meet you both." He turned back to Jim. "Well listen, I won't take up much of your time. I just wanted to make a point of stopping in to see how you're doing. That was quite a hit you took out there."

"Yeah, it was," Jim replied as the grogginess settled back in a little. "I don't know how I'm doing. I just woke up." Both men both turned their heads in unison toward Kenzie, who suddenly looked a little flustered.

"You should probably talk to the doctor," she said.

"Why?" Jim asked. "Hasn't he been in to talk to you guys yet? You don't know how it went?"

"Well, yeah, he has, but I just think the doctor would be able to tell it better than I could.

"Kenzie," Jim said, sounding a little concerned. "Did the surgery go alright?"

"Yes, the surgery went fine. No complications at all." She tried to smile encouragingly.

"But?"

Kenzie's face became somber as she knew she would have to tell him. Maybe if she wished really hard for the doctor to walk in at this moment.

But no such luck.

"It was pretty bad, sweetie," she finally said. She turned her eyes upward as she recalled to mind what the doctor had said. "Both the ACL and the MCL were torn, two of the ligaments in your knee. They've repaired them, but you're going to be out of commission for a while. And it's going to take some rehab."

"How long?" Jim asked softly. "Am I going to miss the rest of the season?"

Kenzie's somber face turned grim.

"Yes."

Jim looked back at Jaworski. His face was also grim.

"What do you think, Mr. Jaworski? You've probably seen lots of injuries like this."

Jaworski nodded. "I've seen a few." He paused, started to speak, and paused again. He had the look of a man trying to be diplomatic. "Well," he finally said, "I'm no doctor, but I do know that's quite an injury." Another pause. "Son, I won't say you'll never play football again, but I'm afraid I *can* say that it's fairly likely. And I will say for a fact that no team would feel very comfortable drafting someone after such a serious injury."

Jim's heart sunk, and Kenzie squeezed his hand.

"I'm so sorry, son," Jaworski said. "It's a damn shame. I hope I'm wrong. I hope you're one of the exceptions. And I wish you the best of luck."

He nodded a goodbye to each of them and quietly slipped out the door, leaving Jim feeling lower than he had ever felt.

"Shit." It was the next day and Jim was out of post-op, in his own room.

"I know, baby. But it's not the end of the world." Kenzie had remained by his side almost constantly. Jim had enjoyed a visit with his family, but they had gone home now.

"It's the end of *mine*!" Jim replied. "I was on the way to going pro. I had a chance to be picked by the New England Patriots!"

"I know," Kenzie said. "I heard."

Jim's eyes filled with tears.

"I don't know what I'm going to do. I can't do anything else. They've been after me for a while to declare a major at school, but I still haven't. I've kept my grades up on my general courses, so I could keep playing football. I've taken a couple of business and finance classes, so I'd know how to manage all the money I was going to make."

Kenzie squeezed his hand, and she felt her own eyes filling with tears.

"I've taken a few art classes," Jim continued, and his voice sounded bleak. "I figured they'd be easy. But I suck at them." He scoffed. "And I think the only reason I took those was because I envied the attention Lainey got for her sculpture. But I don't have anything near her talent or motivation."

He looked at Kenzie and sighed.

"I don't have enough credits in anything to declare a major. And it's going to take me even longer now, being stuck here and in rehab, to build the credits to be able to graduate."

"What are you saying, Jim?"

"I've wasted the last two and a half years," he said bitterly. "And I have nothing to show for it. I can't play football. Can't do anything else. Can't get enough credits to graduate without staying in college at least an additional year or two, which I can't afford." He looked at the blank wall across the room, and he shook his head. "As soon as I'm mobile again, I just need to get out and find a job."

"Well, honey, don't make any major decisions just yet. We might be able to work something out."

"There's nothing to work out. I'm an aimless washout who can't do the one thing I went there to do. I'll just have to get out and join the working force."

Kenzie knew it wouldn't help to keep trying to talk him out of quitting college. He would just rail against her resistance. She just had to be supportive.

"You know I'll be behind you in whatever you decide," she said. After a few seconds of silence, just to keep him talking, she asked, "So, what do you think you'll look for?"

"Whatever I can get. Whatever will make enough money to support my needs."

"*Our* needs," Kenzie said. "And you know I'll help, too."

How much more stolen merchandise do you have stashed away?" Valerie asked angrily. Shannon was still in the same place on the sofa, where she had been when Elliot and Hunter were here.

"A little," Shannon answered softly, reluctantly. "Not that much." Valerie looked at her with building frustration.

"Well, we're going to go through your room and round up all the things you've stolen, and you're going to return them to their rightful owners."

"How am I going to do that, Val?" Shannon asked belligerently. "It's mostly just a little cash here and there. I don't know who I got it from."

Valerie stared at her for a moment.

"Unfuckingbelievable!" she finally spat. That was the moment when Shannon realized how angry Valerie really was. She seldom swore, and when she did, it was usually just a damn or a hell. Never the biggies.

"I'm sorry, Val," Shannon said, striking a more contrite tone. "I am. But we've already been through this, on Saturday when you picked me up at airport security."

"Oh, and wasn't that a proud moment!"

"I know, but you already grounded me for it. Why do we have to go through it again? Doesn't double jeopardy apply?"

"Double jeopardy? No! This is not a democracy. This is my house. You bring stolen merchandise in here, and I'm harboring a criminal, and probably aiding and abetting. Certainly not going to win me 'Mother of the Year'!"

"You're not my mother," Shannon replied, not meaning for it to sound quite as harsh as it did.

"No, I'm not." Valerie scoffed and looked at Shannon, shaking her head. "Wouldn't *she* be proud!"

Shannon looked at her through the tears accumulating in her eyes. Then she got up and went upstairs. Valerie heard her door slam a few seconds later.

Valerie hadn't meant to come off that acerbic, but she knew she had the right. The kid had never been easy, but now she had definitely gone too far.

Shannon lay face down on her bed, her pillow now wet with tears. How had her life gotten so fucked up? Sure, her parents died when she was young, but that wasn't a guarantee of a shitty life. She may be an orphan, but her situation was certainly not Dickensian.

In fact, Val *was* a good mother. She had done the best she could, under the circumstances. When Shannon lost her parents, Val also lost her brother and benefactor. And just a short time before that, she had been married to an abusive asshole of a husband. So she had been through more than her fair share of shit, too.

And Shannon repays her by being a spoiled brat, and a thief. Plus, as a side-effect of her thievery, three of her own friends were now dead. She didn't know how. She knew that Elliot insisted that it wasn't possible, but how else could it be explained? As a weird coincidence, he said.

No. One might be just a coincidence. Two would be stretching it. But three? Not a chance. She knew it had something to do with that computer.

Which again put the responsibility squarely on her shoulders. If she hadn't stolen it, her friends would still be alive.

But then, likely *other* people would be dying and nobody would know about it. In that case, it's almost a good thing that she stole it.

But she knew she was just making excuses. The ends don't justify the means. What the hell was wrong with her?

Well, she knew what was wrong with her. She had already diagnosed herself some time back, after her studies of the human mind and behavior. She suffered from depression, an antisocial personality disorder and passive aggressive self-loathing with kleptomaniac tendencies.

Valerie was right. Shannon's mother would be *so* proud!

As the afternoon light through her window cast long, dark shadows into her room, Shannon fell asleep, thinking of the people and the life that she had lost.

It always started out the same.

Shannon was straining against the seat belt. Strapped into the back seat, she pushed herself up with her hands as much as she could, tilting her head back to see out the window. There really wasn't much to see, though. Just trees rushing by at the side of the highway. She relaxed, sinking back into the seat and brushing her raven hair out of her eyes.

Her parents had said she would see Valerie soon. She always liked going to Valerie's place. The creek rushing past the back of her house often attracted deer, and sometimes even a bighorn sheep. Shannon loved animals.

She looked down at Kitty, a plush black panther, and she picked it up. She didn't have a real pet, but she enjoyed petting the stuffed toy. It was soft, and its fur felt so smooth against her little fingers.

She heard voices in the front seat, but she didn't know what was being said. She usually didn't pay any attention to grownup talk. She didn't understand it. It was always so boring.

"Pretty Kitty," she muttered to the toy, brushing its fur back on its face. She began rocking her head, her hair swinging back and forth to the rhythm as she chanted, "Pretty Kitty, Pretty Kitty, Pretty Kitty . . ."

She heard an exclamation from the front seat, but since she couldn't see out the windows, she didn't know what was happening. But she felt the seat belt and shoulder belt suddenly press into her body as the brakes were being applied aggressively, and she heard the tires squeal on the pavement.

There was a brief swerve, then a hard jolt and a thunderous noise as the car was hit by another. Shannon could see and hear what was happening, as if in slow motion, but only in her little area. Kitty fell onto the floor of the car, and Shannon glanced briefly at it, but her attention was immediately drawn back to the noise and the dizzying feeling of the car spinning in a circle.

Shannon thought she heard a scream from the front seat, but she wasn't sure. There was so much noise, so many different sounds at once.

Looking up to her window, the sky disappeared as the blur of a big truck's trailer appeared, and the car slid under it with a deafening crash. Little pebbles rained down all around her as the glass shattered. She was jerked to the side as the car suddenly stopped spinning.

And the scream stopped.

Shannon felt something in her lap, but it was dark now, as the bottom of the trailer was only about an inch above her. In a moment, her eyes adjusted to the dim light shining through what was left of the window on the other side of the car.

She looked down in her lap and saw her mother's head.

The block of walnut, clamped to the top of Lainey's work bench, was roughly fourteen inches wide, fourteen inches deep and about two feet tall. The dark wood, almost a purplish brown, was unmarked, with tight, slightly diagonal grain and a fine texture.

Lainey studied the block from her wheelchair, carefully scrutinizing the wood. She subscribed to Michelangelo's philosophy of sculpture. He once said, "Every block of stone has a statue inside it and it is the task of the sculptor to discover it." Lainey felt that the same ideology applied to a block of wood. So before she put any tools to the block, she always spent some time really looking at it, visually tracing the direction of the grain, taking note of color variations.

She sometimes made rough sketches of what she wanted to carve, but usually her work was improvised, with the bulk of the design being done in this preliminary stage.

But Lainey's work bench was a little high to see the block comfortably while seated in her wheelchair, so she pushed herself up. She wasn't continually confined to the chair yet, but she tired quickly. So the chair was usually nearby.

Leaning against the bench, having examined the block to her satisfaction, she picked up her mallet and a straight gouge with a wide blade. She placed the blade of the gouge on top of the block, waiting for her hand to steady, and positioned it carefully on the end grain. She tipped the blade a bit, until it was slanted just right, parallel with the curve of the grain, and she rapped the handle with the mallet. She moved the blade a little to one side and rapped it again.

A few more carefully-placed cuts, and a large, curving section separated from the block. Lainey put the gouge and the mallet down and tugged the waste chunk off of the block, tearing it away from the grain fibers that still connected them.

Already tired from her activities, she lowered herself back into her chair. It had been two years since her diagnosis, and it was becoming more difficult for her to cope with her increasing disability. The patience and positive attitude that Kenzie and Jim had teased her about that day were in shorter supply.

But she couldn't let herself think about that for very long. She did what she needed to do to address her symptoms, and to cope with her infirmities, and then she forced her mind onto more positive thoughts.

She focused on the walnut again. Looking at the shape of the block and the direction of the grain, she discovered the statue inside it, and she smiled.

Elliot was not happy. Sitting in front of his computer, examining the files he had copied from Shannon's computer was starting to get to him. Scanning millions of lines of computer code was tedious work. But he had willingly done it numerous times. That wasn't why he was unhappy. He had said repeatedly that it's not possible to poke someone in Facebook and have them turn up dead from a stab wound. And yet they wanted him to waste hours trying to find how it was done anyway – that's what was making him crazy!

Why hire an expert consultant, and then completely disregard everything he says?

But then, they didn't hire him. He was doing this as a favor to Hunter.

Shit.

And not just Hunter, but Shannon, too. Damn, that girl was gorgeous!

He remembered the last time he let an infatuation leverage his work. It was four years ago. He was only eighteen at the time, Shannon's age, riddled with hormones and easily influenced by attention from the opposite sex.

Dani Eisen was a pretty blonde whom Elliot knew from a couple of his college classes. She was particularly passionate in biology, outspoken about conservation issues.

One day, when her computer was giving her problems in class, and she was balking at filing a service request with the IT department and waiting for it to be processed, Elliot made a couple of quick adjustments and got it working for her. She was impressed, and thankful.

Elliot was now on her radar.

He had noticed her watching him a few times after that, when he was busy examining code, which confounded everyone but the complete nerds in his computer class. It was a couple of weeks later that she approached him in the library with a proposal.

"Are you a hacker?" Dani asked.

"I've done a little," Elliot replied. It was the truth, but he hoped his tone made him sound modest instead of inexperienced.

"Could you hack the Department of the Interior for me?"

"Huh?"

"The Department of the Interior. It's a section of the government devoted, among other things, to natural resources and energy supplies."

"I know what it is," Elliot said. "But who the hell hacks the Department of the Interior?"

It was Dani's turn to act confused.

"The Department of Defense?" Elliot went on. "Sure. The Energy grid? You bet. Air Traffic Control? Absolutely!

NSA? CIA? All worthy goals. I've seen all of them attempted to varying degrees of success in the movies.

"But the Department of the Interior?"

"What? You think it's beneath you?" Dani asked.

"No, I just think it's weird."

Dani sighed, then huddled up close to him.

"Okay," she said, "here's the thing. I'm a member of a local conservation group, a kind of grass roots watchdog organization."

"I never would have guessed."

"Whatever. Anyway, we suspect the DoI is suppressing a study about the Preble's meadow jumping mouse."

"The what?"

"The Preble's meadow jumping mouse. It's an endangered species. It's only known to exist in parts of Colorado and Wyoming."

"Okay, so why would the Interior be suppressing this report? It's an endangered animal. Isn't this little varmint right up their alley?"

"Conflict of interest," Dani explained. "The Department of the Interior is also about energy. And we think they're suppressing this study about the Preble in favor of a new hydroelectric dam project."

"Ah," Elliot said as the pieces came together. "The country needs more clean energy, but who gives a shit about a mouse?"

"Exactly."

"I don't know, though," Elliot said shaking his head. "I've never hacked the government before. I mean the Department of the Interior, it's not a sexy hack, but it's still the US Government."

"You won't do it?"

"I'd be taking quite a risk. I think my compensation should be proportionate."

"You did hear me say that we're a local grass roots conservation group, right? We don't exactly have deep pockets."

Elliot resisted the idea, hesitant to get involved. Dani leaned toward him as if she was going to whisper something to him. Instead, he felt her warm breath as her tongue traced the whorls and contours of his ear. She knew he got the point when he shivered.

A few moments of fingertip negotiations, and they gathered up their books and left.

The night at her place was alternately spent talking about the Preble, sleeping and making love. In retrospect, Elliot realized that Dani would probably have thought of it as just fucking. And maybe that's all it was. But Elliot was a little more moved by it than that. The result was the same, though. Dani proved to be pretty persuasive.

As it turned out, Elliot was able to do the hack easily enough. The government must have thought the same thing – who hacks the Department of the Interior? The server's safeguards were fairly easy to get past.

But once he was in, he couldn't find any trace of the suppressed mouse study. Dani kept urging him deeper, trying to get him to keep looking. But after a while, Elliot was getting nervous with the amount of time he had been in already. He called it quits, getting him a look of disdain from Dani.

She left and they never spoke again. Elliot knew he had been used, but he didn't care.

Not until the feds showed up at his door.

There was no evidence of any files actually being taken, so the charges were fairly minimal. It was easy enough to negotiate immunity in exchange for the people who put him up to it.

He hesitated, at first, particularly about Dani. But they used him, and he was the one to get caught. He divulged the name of the group without naming Dani specifically.

They were mentioned a few times in the news after that, but again, since no files were actually stolen, the case eventually just petered out.

Looking now at his computer screen, at the lines of code blurring together, he felt as if he had been used again.

And Shannon hadn't even touched him.

H ow happy are you?" Lainey asked slowly, concentrating on her pronunciation. "Really?" Kenzie looked at her sitting in her wheelchair, her body curved a little bit to one side. They were in Lainey's workshop, in April of 2008.

"I'm fine, Lainey," Kenzie insisted. "Really!"

Lainey's mouth had a slight permanent curve applied to it that, to someone who didn't know her, might look like a sneer. Kenzie was able to see past that, and see the expression of disbelief on her friend's face.

In the seven years since she had been diagnosed, the disease had made occasional advancements, interspersed with periods of apparent dormancy. Lainey now spent most of her time in her wheelchair. Her legs no longer had the strength to support her for very long, even with her crutches.

"You've been married for a year," Lainey replied, "and I hardly ever see the old sweet, bubbly Kenzie anymore. Just glimpses once in a while."

"Well, you just said it yourself, Lainey" Kenzie said, a little more forcefully than she intended, "I've been married for a year. The honeymoon never lasts forever. I'm just living real life now. The daily grind doesn't really allow somebody to always be deliriously happy. We've got bills. We've got jobs. Just the usual stuff we have to deal with. But I'm fine."

"The lady doth protest too much," Lainey replied. The 'sneer' moved slightly as Lainey's gaze, more piercing now, took in Kenzie's demeanor. Kenzie was almost getting to the point of being uncomfortable under her stare, when Lainey finally spoke again. "I know Jimmy can be hard to live with sometimes."

"He's fine, Lainey," Kenzie said dismissively, looking down at the floor.

"He's a fucking asshole!" Lainey said raising her voice. Kenzie quickly looked up at Lainey, who seemed to register a bit of embarrassment. "Sorry," she sighed. "MS sometimes causes what they diplomatically call unstable moods."

"I know, sweetie," Kenzie said. "It's okay." She had seen a few instances of Lainey's uncharacteristic short-temper. Familiar with her usual upbeat, positive attitude, Kenzie let it slide.

"I lived with Jimmy for years," Lainey continued, struggling to keep her voice even. "I know he can be a controlling bastard. And I'm afraid I'm seeing the effects in you now."

"It's true," Kenzie said slowly, treading carefully, "he likes things a certain way. But that's the way it is with pretty much everybody."

Kenzie was anxious to change the subject, as Lainey's comments were actually hitting close to home. Jim had taken control of most facets of their home life. Early on, they had started pooling their income into a joint account. Recently, he had taken control of the account, allotting specific amounts of money for different expenses. If Kenzie needed more money for something than had been given to her, she had to ask Jim for it.

"I'm sorry I introduced you," Lainey said quietly.

"What are you working on?" Kenzie asked, hoping to distract Lainey with a different topic. "I see you have something on your bench, but I haven't seen it without the cover in a while."

Lainey's dad had cut the legs off of her work bench a couple of years before, so that the work surface was easier for her to reach from her wheelchair. Even so, she seldom had the energy to work for very long.

The project clamped to the bench had a blanket tossed over it. Lainey still occasionally worked on other projects. Small commissions were the only ones she would accept anymore. But when not working on a paying commission, she would work on this pet project when she was able.

"It's a secret project," Lainey said.

"A secret? Cool! What is it? Who's it for?"

"What part of 'secret' did you not understand?" Her tone was quiet and stern, but Kenzie could see a trace of the smile on Lainey's face.

"Okay," Kenzie conceded. "Is it a commission, or is it a sculpture you're doing for yourself?"

"I'm doing it for a friend," Lainey said. She looked up at the dirty blanket covering it and sighed. "I'm afraid I can't work on it as much as I would like. I started it a few years ago, but I can only manage a few minutes at a time until I can't control my tools any longer."

When she turned back to Kenzie, there were tears in her eyes. Kenzie's heart ached for her.

"Honey, I'm so sorry," she said. She forced herself to project a positive tone. "But you're such a gifted artist. It's like your hands are connected directly to your heart. It may take you longer to do the work now, but I know that, as always, it will still be beautiful. Because it came from your heart."

Lainey closed her eyes for a moment, sending the tears tumbling down her cheeks. When she opened them again, she was able to move the 'sneer' into an actual smile.

"I love you, Kenzie," she whispered.

"I love you too, Lainey," Kenzie said, as her own eyes filled with tears.

She quickly brushed them away as she heard a sound behind her. The door to Lainey's workshop opened and Jim came in.

"Come on, Kenzie," he said. "We need to go."

"Okay, Jim. I'll be right there."

She noticed the smile faded from Lainey's face. Kenzie leaned over and kissed her cheek, then she followed Jim out the door.

Shannon sat on her bed with the computer open on her lap. She felt a messy knot of feelings about the machine – fear, fascination, disgust. Disbelief.

She knew it was a crazy notion, that some innocuous little Facebook command, a lighthearted little 'poke,' could make a person end up dead. It was the stuff of science fiction. So yes, she also felt a little disbelief.

As Valerie's friend, Hunter, had told Elliot, "We're open to other ideas, but at the moment, they ain't presenting themselves. And the only thing we can think of for now is the computer."

In a way, she hoped that Elliot *would* say for certain that it's not the computer. To think that something that everybody uses on a daily basis could somehow magically turn deadly was just too scary.

At the same time, that would leave them with no explanation of how her three friends, separated by all that distance, and with no other apparent connection, could all be killed the same way, in about three days' time. There had to be an explanation. She just couldn't figure out what it could be.

But she was trying, not just because the question was so puzzling. She was also trying desperately to forget the dream that had awoken her a little while before. And not only the dream, but the memory that it opened up.

She assumed that the recent trauma of losing her friends in quick succession had revealed an earlier trauma that she had previously been unable to face. But was she able to face it now? Remembering the surprised expression on her mother's face as her severed head lay in five-year-old Shannon's lap, she could feel the tears coming to her eyes again.

When Shannon woke up screaming hysterically, Valerie had been here in seconds, her arms around her, trying to calm her. After Shannon had regained her composure enough to relate the dream and memory, Valerie's own face reflected the shock and horror of what Shannon had endured. Apparently Valerie had not known all the gory details of the accident herself.

Valerie had spent at least a half hour holding Shannon, quietly rocking her back and forth as if she were a little child. And Shannon had been surprised to find that she didn't mind that. Quite the contrary, in fact, it felt soothing and comforting. It didn't remove the horror of what had happened to her, but it did help to ease the distress of the memory.

What she was left with was something she hadn't felt in a while, that of truly belonging. Valerie was family.

Shannon and Valerie had grown apart over the years. She knew that. She also knew that it was largely her own fault. That realization was disarming. She knew her look and her lifestyle pushed people away. But it was more than that. She recognized that she had actively excluded Valerie from her life.

When Valerie was holding her so tightly, attempting to soothe her, Shannon realized how much she had missed it. And she desperately wanted to get it back.

Even though she wasn't ready to give up her goth friends, the ones who were still alive anyway, or her unconventional look, she did resolve to be a better niece and friend to Valerie.

To be better family.

She noticed it had gotten dark and she reached over to turn on the lamp. In the past, she loved sitting in the dark, whether browsing Facebook or listening to her music. After the dream revived her memory of the accident, she welcomed light.

She looked back at the computer and decided to put it away. She hadn't reached any conclusions about it, and it didn't seem to do any good to sit there and stare at it.

Before she could shut it down, she heard the ping of a private message. She went to the private messages page in Facebook, and saw that the message was from Elliot. She smiled, the memory of his face, his beautiful blue eyes, warming her.

"It's not the computer," he said. "Must be some other explanation. Don't worry."

Almost immediately, she received a notice that she had been poked. It was from Elliot.

She looked at the notice with some trepidation. At the same time, she was reminded of the somewhat sexual nuance that she associated with poking someone, particularly a man. Just the thought that 'Elliot poked me' caused a warm sensation deep inside her.

It's not the computer. It was a relief to see that. But still, there was a certain lack of closure. If not the computer, then what?

But at least they knew now that the problem lay somewhere else. Definitely a relief!

She returned the poke.

Elliot felt good now that he was out from under the burden of trying to find a non-existent digital murder weapon. The whole idea was ludicrous. He understood that they were desperate to find something to blame. But those people had real, physical killers. *They're* the ones to blame.

He still felt bad in a way, though. He had worded his message to Shannon in a way that implied he had finished looking at all the code and didn't find an offending file. The fact was that he had just quit. No need wasting his time searching for something that he knew didn't exist.

He was hoping that, now that he wasn't tied to that activity, he could get down to the business of flirting with Shannon. He wanted to spend some serious time with her, *not* related to computer issues.

Before he could, though, his phone rang. It was Hunter.

Fuck!

"Hi Hunter," he answered, trying not to sound as unhappy to hear from him as he felt.

"Hey, Elliot," Hunter drawled. "How you doing, son?"

"Fine."

"Just wanted to check and see how the computer examination is going."

"I'm done," Elliot replied. "It's not the computer."

"You're done already?" Elliot held his breath, hoping that would be the end of it. He let it out as Hunter continued. "But I thought it was going to take a long time for you to look at all those lines of code. It's only been, what, about three hours?"

Elliot sighed, preparing to embark upon his explanation one more time.

"Hunter, it's Facebook. A stupid Facebook poke doesn't kill someone."

"I agree. But why them? And why, directly after Shannon poked them?"

Elliot didn't have an answer for that, but Hunter didn't leave time for a response anyway.

"Elliot, like I said earlier, we're open to other ideas. We're stuck on this right now because it just seems like too much of a coincidence. But if you got another idea, I'd love to hear it."

"Those victims were killed by real people," Elliot replied, "not by some string of computer code."

"I understand that, son. But why? What did they have in common? Why were they targeted?"

"I don't know, Hunter. But I don't see how my spending hours reading millions of lines of computer code is going to answer that."

"I don't either. And I ain't going to force you to do it. But I do wish you could put yourself in my position. It didn't matter to me personally if your daddy was cleared of the charges against him or not. But it mattered to you."

Elliot started feeling like a major shit.

"I know that Valerie and Shannon don't mean anything to *you* personally," Hunter continued, "but they're my friends. And Shannon's lost three of her friends recently. She's the one suffering the most. But I got nothing to tell her. No way to ease her mind about this. No explanation at all. I mean, do you really think that three people killed in three days after being poked is nothing but a coincidence? Would *you* be satisfied with that explanation?"

"Probably not," Elliot conceded quietly.

"Then eliminate this as a possibility. Don't just *say* it ain't the code. Prove it."

"Alright, Hunter," Elliot sighed, a tone of shame in his voice, "I'll get back into it."

"Thank you, Elliot. I really do appreciate it. And maybe once this is all over, I can do something to make it worth your while."

They disconnected and Elliot sat back down heavily in front of his computer.

He had started with the smaller files he had copied from Shannon's computer. If there *was* anything to find, he hoped it would be in one of them.

But he came up empty.

Unable to put it off any longer, he opened up the source code for the Chrome browser. For comparison purposes, he opened up a copy of it from his own computer as well, so he could look at his own and Shannon's side by side.

He took a deep breath, blew it out noisily, then started scanning through the code.

Elliot had been looking at lines of Chrome source code for about two hours, when something unusual caught his eye. He wasn't sure what to make of it. He looked down at the clock on the taskbar. It was just after nine o'clock. After all the tedious code comparison he'd been doing, it seemed later than that.

He rubbed his eyes and leaned forward, looking at the lines in question. There was nothing like it in his copy of Chrome. In fact, he'd never seen anything like it before. He hated to admit it, but they may have actually been right.

Aside from that regret he felt at his outspokenness against this whole idea, though, he was also thrilled. This was something new, something exciting.

Dangerous, yes, downright deadly! But that's partly what made it so exciting.

He could hardly wait to tell someone.

I'm man enough to admit I was wrong." Shannon puckered her brows as she looked at Elliot's message. "I did find something after all. Too much to write here, though."

She wondered what he had found. And she wondered what its impact would be considering the fact that she had poked him. With this computer!

She was about to respond when she heard Valerie urgently calling her.

"Shannon, come downstairs right now, please!"

"Great," she thought, "now what?" She looked at the message for a moment, then, with a sigh, she pushed the computer aside. She'll take care of whatever Valerie wants, then chat with Elliot when she can concentrate on the conversation.

As she reached the bottom of the stairs, she saw a man in a suit standing at the door with Valerie.

"Are you Shannon York?" he asked.

"Yeah?" Shannon replied. It came out like a question.

"I'm Detective Hardison with the Colorado Springs Police Department." He showed his badge. "Ms. York, you've been named as a person of interest in our investigation of the murder of Kaley Angeli. I'd like to ask you some questions."

Valerie looked at Shannon. Shannon noticed that she looked especially tired.

"I didn't kill Kaley," Shannon said. "She was my friend. And I wasn't even down there."

"Where were you at about 7:45 this morning?" Detective Hardison asked.

"I was upstairs, asleep."

Detective Hardison glanced at Valerie, who nodded.

"That's right," she said. "I was here. Shannon came downstairs at about ten o'clock."

The detective jotted something down in a notebook.

"Why have you come all the way up here to ask about this?" Valerie asked.

"I'm just following up on some clues," he replied obliquely. "Ms. York," he said, turning his attention back to Shannon, "you were Facebook friends with Ms. Angeli, correct?"

"Yes," Shannon answered, feeling her eyes suddenly burn.

The detective turned a couple of pages back in his notebook. "We've been looking for any clues in her Facebook activity. You told Ms. Angeli, 'two people I poked in the last two days are dead. Be careful, don't be alone, call the police.' Why did you tell her that?"

"Seriously?" Shannon asked incredulously. "Because two people I poked are dead. I was worried about Kaley."

"I'm not really sure I understand how your actions affected them," Hardison replied, "but we *are* curious about those people, and about your connection to them. We checked out the two names you mentioned, Kevin Morgan and Jenny Lynne, and found reports of their very similar murders."

"The Colorado Springs Police Department must be a model of efficiency," Shannon said. "Kaley was killed this morning, and you're already looking at her Facebook activity. Don't you question witnesses first?"

"There weren't any witnesses," Hardison replied. "And her brother, Eddy, mentioned your warning to us. Kaley was kind of scared by what you told her and she confided in him. Eddy's the one who told her the whole thing was a silly idea. He's also the one who remembered it when we were at the scene this morning."

"So," Shannon said, "somebody *finally* sees a link between these murders without me having to convince them. And now I'm a suspect?"

"No, miss, you're not a suspect. I said you've been named as a person of interest."

"What's the difference?"

"Person of interest simply means that you are someone who may possess information that might assist us in our investigation." Hardison glanced at Valerie and back at Shannon. "Also, I'm not officially investigating the Morgan and Lynne murders, since they're out of my jurisdiction. I'm only trying to determine if there *is* any kind of link between those crimes and the murder of Kaley Angeli."

"There is," Shannon said matter-of-factly. "That's what I've been trying to tell everyone."

"I know it's a long shot," Hardison said, "but I assume you can account for your whereabouts at the times of these other murders?"

"She was here," Valerie said. "She's been here for the last four days. She's – " Valerie glanced at Shannon. "She's grounded." Shannon rolled her eyes.

"Why's that?"

"What the fuck does it matter to *you* why I'm grounded?" Shannon demanded. "You really think that has any bearing on your fucking case?"

"Look, Detective," Valerie quickly said before Hardison could respond, "we were just talking to a private detective and a computer expert a few hours ago about Shannon's suspicions concerning that computer."

"What computer?"

"The laptop computer I used to kill those people," Shannon retorted.

"Shannon!" Valerie exclaimed.

"That reminds me," Shannon continued undeterred, "I need to get back to Elliot. He just sent me a message. He thinks he found something."

"Really?" Valerie asked, momentarily taken aback.

"Okay," Hardison said, shifting impatiently from one foot to the other, "one of you want to fill me in on whatever the hell you're talking about?"

"Shannon's had her suspicions about this computer," Valerie sighed, "and after Kaley was killed this morning, we called Hunter Sage, a private investigator in Denver, and he brought a computer expert, Elliot Logan, with him. Shannon related to them what you already know, about her poking these people and how they ended up dead."

"And how did her computer acquire this magical ability to kill people?" Hardison asked sarcastically.

"It's – " Valerie looked at Shannon again. Shannon shrugged, a bored expression on her face, though under the surface, she was anxious to talk more to Elliot. "It's not hers," Valerie continued. "It's stolen."

Hardison looked at Shannon with one eyebrow raised. Again, Shannon rolled her eyes.

"How is it that in five minutes of talking with you two, I know less than I did about this case than when I got here?"

"I guess they just don't make detectives like they used to," Shannon replied.

"Shannon, please!" The tired look was back on Valerie's face, and Shannon felt a tinge of regret.

"Can I see this killer laptop?" Hardison asked.

"What do you think you're going to learn from looking at it?" Shannon asked. "It's just a laptop."

"Humor me, okay?"

Shannon sighed and plodded back up the stairs. She returned a few moments later carrying the computer. She held it up beside her face in a sarcastic Vanna White pose.

"See? Just a computer."

Hardison took it and looked at it, turning it over.

"And you stole this?" he asked.

Shannon looked at him for a moment.

"Yes, I stole it," she finally said defiantly.

"Don't worry," Hardison replied. "I'm not a larceny investigator. I'm in homicide. But I *am* going to have to confiscate this as evidence in our investigation."

"Wait, no," Shannon said. "Elliot may need to see it again, now that he's found something."

"Let him take it," Valerie said. "It'll be a relief to be rid of it."

"And this Elliot Logan," Hardison said. "I assume he's in Denver too? I think I'd like to talk with him."

old on, son," Hunter said, his cell phone pressed tightly against his ear. He and Kenzie were just about to go to bed, and he waved her on when he realized the call was going to take a while. "So you're saying you *did* find something wonky on that little girl's computer?"

"Yeah!" Elliot enthused. "It's incredible! I mean, don't get me wrong, it's some bad shit, but it's pure evil genius!"

Hunter sat rigid on the sofa. He couldn't work himself up to feeling quite as giddy about it as Elliot was.

"Okay," he said, "why don't you tell me what you found."

"There's this private group on Facebook called Swift Poker. Sounds pretty innocuous, like a group of card lovers or something. I haven't been able to find it on Facebook yet, so I don't know how they get their members, if they recruit them or if the members somehow seek them out.

"But just from what this plug-in does, I can only assume the group is for jilted lovers or racists or somebody who wants revenge. Basically, anybody who has trouble dealing with people in a civilized way."

"Wait," Hunter interrupted. "Plug-in? What are you talking about?"

"A plug-in is a component, a bit of code that adds features to an already existing application. You install it on your computer and it starts working in conjunction with the application that it's made for. You're probably familiar with the Adobe Flash Player or the QuickTime Player. They're well-known plug-ins that add functionality to a web browser."

"Oh, okay. Gotcha."

"So this plug-in works in the Chrome browser in conjunction with Facebook. I assume that every member of Swift Poker is given a copy of the plug-in to install on their computer."

"So, what does this plug-in do?"

"From what I've been able to figure out so far, its purpose is fourfold. First, when somebody who has that plug-in pokes somebody in Facebook, the plug-in sends an encrypted message to the group, or maybe just to somebody local, I'm not sure yet. But the recipient gets information about the person who was poked – their name, where they live, other pertinent details. It even gathers photos from their Facebook profile and sends them along to help identify them.

"The algorithm necessary to get the stuff that's already gathered together on Facebook is a fairly basic one. But it goes beyond that by getting the target's exact address, either from the location feature on their phone, if they use that, or people finder web sites.

"I can't find anything in the plug-in concerning what the recipient is expected to do with this information, but considering what we've heard from Shannon, apparently they're supposed to follow through by stabbing that person to death. Poking them for real."

"Damn, son, that's crazy!"

"No shit!"

"Wait," Hunter said, "you can only poke friends, right? Why would somebody you hate enough to kill be one of your Facebook friends?"

"Actually, I was coming to that. That's the second thing the plug-in does. It transcends the friend barrier. If somebody is on Facebook, they can be poked.

"The third thing the plug-in does is hide the IP address and location of the computer it's working on. It acts like a digital cloaking device, protecting the owner of the computer from any implication in wrongdoing. And fourth, it keeps the members of the group from having any actual incriminating contact with each other."

"You mean we can't find who belongs to the group?" Hunter asked, feeling disappointed.

"No, not through the plug-in, anyway. You'd probably have to subpoena Facebook to get that information.

"But judging by the name of the group, and by what Shannon told us about the three cases she knew, they're apparently supposed to follow through quickly. Get in, get the job done, and get out.

"If you think about it, there's also some protection in the fact that the person who actually kills the victim is not the same person that poked them. There's no connection. It's kind of like that old Hitchcock movie, *Strangers on a Train*. There's nothing that ties the killer to the victim. It simply appears to be a random killing.

"And there's also nothing that ties the victim to the person that poked them. The person who initiated the hit is protected by the fact that he's not the one who did the deed. In fact, he could be thousands of miles away."

"Okay," Hunter said. "Let's keep this quiet. We don't want any of the members getting wind that we're onto them and have them abandon the group before we can get them. I'll contact my friend at the FBI and fill him in on what you told me, and see about getting a subpoena for the members of that Facebook group.

"Maybe you should let Shannon know, too."

"I did. I sent her a message that I found something. I didn't go into detail, though. I needed to tell somebody, but I was excited and it was too much to type out.

"I know she saw my message, but she still hasn't responded – oh shit!"

"What is it?"

"I just remembered. She poked me."

"What?" Hunter felt a knot of apprehension growing in his chest.

"It was before you called me earlier. I didn't think there was anything to it, no way the killings could be connected to the computer. So I told her it wasn't the computer, and to make the point that I was sure of it, I poked her. She poked me back a couple of minutes later."

Hunter was already up and gathering his keys and his gun.

"Okay, you stay put, son," he said. "It'll take me about twenty minutes to get up there. You stay inside and keep your door locked. If you hear anybody before I get there, call 911 right away, you got me?"

"Yeah," Elliot replied, the excitement he was previously feeling noticeably absent now from his voice.

Hunter disconnected as Kenzie came out of the bathroom wearing a short teddy, her luxurious red hair spilling down over her shoulders. Hunter looked at her and sighed.

"Damn, honey!" he said. "I have to go. You go on to bed without me. I'll try to be back as soon as I can."

Before she could respond, he was gone.

He drove east on Colfax Avenue, past the lights of downtown Denver on his left. He thought traffic still seemed a little heavy considering it was almost ten-thirty on a Tuesday night. Three blocks past the illuminated gold dome of the Colorado Capitol Building directly on his right, he arrived at Pennsylvania Street, and he made a right turn. Not far from the corner, he found an empty parking space.

He got out of his car and looked at the building. It was a brick building, built somewhere around the 1920s or 30s. There were a few interesting architectural details, although the building appeared a little neglected. But it was the right address.

There was a streetlight nearby, so he could easily see where he needed to go. He was aware, though, of all the deep shadows that were cast by the brick pilasters and other architectural elements of the building, and by the trees in front. The neighboring buildings on either side of it were close together, too, separated by only eight or ten feet.

Lots of places for someone to hide.

He went to the front door and stepped into the lighted vestibule. The inner door was locked. He glanced at the mailboxes, and he saw the name, Elliot Logan.

He heard a sound outside. In fact, it was so quiet, he wasn't even sure it *was* a sound. Only the impression of a sound. But it just seemed a little out of place. He stepped back outside.

He stood perfectly still and listened. Then he heard it. It sounded like a slow, stealthy footstep on gravel, coming from the shadows between the buildings.

He stood in the shadow of a tree for a moment, giving his eyes a little time to grow accustomed to the dark again after being in the vestibule. He wished he had brought a flashlight with him, but maybe enough light will filter in there from the streetlight.

It was probably nothing anyway. Just a tenant, or maybe a pedestrian cutting through there from the street to the alley.

He stepped around the corner of the building and came face to face with a shadow.

"Shit!" he heard the shadow say. It sounded as surprised as he was.

He was also surprised by the unusual feeling of pressure on his chest. The pressure passed in just a second, though, and was followed by an intense pain.

He took a step back and felt the blade slide back out of his chest. He felt the warmth of his blood as it ran down the front of his shirt, but the blood was already cooling in the night air as he toppled over.

The shadows enveloped him as the sound of the footsteps faded away.

Billy Liebermann was not having a good night. His assignment had caused almost a feeling of terror from the moment he first received it. Why the hell did he ever join that group?

Well, of course he knew why he joined it. It had been good when his fucking slut of an ex-wife, Sheila, had died in a tragic random act of violence. No more alimony for her. And no more of Billy's leftovers for Brad, her new fuck-buddy.

Yeah, that had been the good part. But he had never given much thought to having to actually carry out a poking himself. Or rather, he had, but he thought it would be easier. Just another hunt.

But it wasn't like hunting. People were more intelligent than a deer or elk. Or more devious.

And if he got caught, it wouldn't be nearly as easy as just producing a hunting license, or proving his gun was properly registered. He could go to prison for a very long time.

So he couldn't get caught. Simple as that.

When the assignment came through, he managed to get past the negative aspects of belonging to Swift Poker. He worked up his courage and went to the target's location.

Then, as he's scouting the premises, he was surprised by a man coming around the corner. Billy almost pissed his pants!

He hadn't meant to stab the guy. It was just a reflex reaction of being scared shitless.

Billy had almost given up and gone home then. He stood in the shadows, running scenarios through his mind. Having a random dead guy lying around could make it more dangerous for him.

But then he realized that going home tonight would likely also prevent him from carrying out his assignment later. Police would be crawling all over this place tomorrow, after the body was found.

And his target might get spooked after that. It could be days before Billy had another shot at it.

He decided to follow through on his assignment. He dragged the body a couple of feet, so that it was in the passage between the buildings. As dark as the shadows were, nobody would find it until morning.

He had already located the exact apartment, and he knew the target was still up. It was a dreary little basement apartment, dimly lit, and Billy had seen him through the window, sitting in front of a computer.

The problem was that there were bars on all of the basement windows.

He decided to do what he had started when he had been interrupted, make a circuit of the building. He went toward the front, cautiously stepping around where he knew the body was. It was so dark, he could barely see it. He carefully looked in all directions before stepping out.

The front basement windows were barred, too. The front door was not a likely entry, unless he just happened to be there when somebody was arriving or leaving and could slip in before the door closed.

The north side of the building was equally shaded and hidden, and with bars on those windows as well. There was a small parking lot behind the building, and a back door. It was a heavy metal door, but the latch looked pretty old. It didn't seem as secure as the front door.

Billy decided that was a possibility. The most likely he had seen so far. He would continue around and finish his circuit, and make sure the target was still in the apartment, and after eliminating all other possible points of entry, he would work on getting in through the back door.

Elliot had been freaked out ever since he realized that he was probably a target now.

Shannon had responded to his private message just after he had spoken with Hunter. She anxiously reminded him that she had poked him, which further freaked him out. Yes, he remembered! She felt better when he told her that Hunter was on his way.

"Stay put," Hunter had said. No shit! He wasn't stepping foot outside his apartment until Hunter got there. Feeling anxious, Elliot decided he needed to focus his attention on something else.

He kept examining the code of the Swift Poker plug-in. And that wasn't helping. What he had found so fascinating just a few minutes before was now terrifying.

He could be killed tonight, stabbed to death, and nobody would have to answer for it. Or at least that's the way it would have been. Now that Hunter knew what was going on, Elliot's murder would be solved.

That was little comfort to Elliot, though. The more optimum alternative, he decided, would be to prevent his murder from ever happening in the first place.

He got up and walked a few steps to his 'efficiency' kitchen. He unscrewed the cap from the Jim Beam bottle on the counter and swallowed a slug of bourbon. As it warmed its way down to his stomach, he felt himself relax a little.

Elliot decided to see if the bourbon would keep doing its job if he continued studying the plug-in. He sat back down at his computer and examined the code. Just a minute or so later, he discovered another feature of the plug-in. Another feature that made him afraid. But not for himself this time.

That was when he noticed the time on the taskbar of his computer. It was a half hour since Hunter had said it would take him twenty minutes to get here.

Hunter couldn't find a place to park and quickly drove around the block. As he came back around, he impatiently pulled into the parking lot behind the Chinese restaurant on the corner and skidded into the nearest space. He jumped out of his car and ran diagonally across the street toward Elliot's building.

As he sprinted toward the front door, something caught his eye at the side of the building, something he probably wouldn't have even seen if the headlights from a passing car hadn't cast a little peripheral light there. It looked like the feet of someone lying on the ground.

He approached cautiously, hoping that Elliot hadn't disregarded his order to stay put. He pulled his Glock 22 from its holster as he got closer, but the light had faded as the car disappeared down the street. The passage between the buildings was pitch black.

Hunter peeked around the corner before walking into the passage. Then, with his free hand, he got his cell phone and hit the button to wake it up. The light from its screen illuminated the body of a man in a suit. The front of his shirt was soaked in blood.

Hunter knelt down beside the man and felt for a pulse. Finding none, he next checked for identification. He found a shoulder holster, and a badge. Detective Hardison, from the Colorado Springs Police Department.

Hunter's first thought was of Shannon's friend, Kaley, in Colorado Springs. Could Detective Hardison be here about that? Or was it just a coincidence?

He didn't take the time to try to figure out the answer. He heard a muted sound from the back of the building, metal on metal. He turned his phone off, plunging himself into darkness. The only light in the passage was from a basement window ahead, which he thought was about where Elliot's apartment was, and moonlight in the back parking lot.

Hunter walked slowly, carefully, trying to disturb the gravel as little as possible. As he came near to the corner of the building, he looked into the parking lot. There was a street light in the alley near it, but the bulb had been shattered. He crept closer and peeked around.

He heard the sound again as he saw a man at the back door, trying to slip the blade of a dagger under the metal guard on the security door.

"Something I can help you with?" Hunter said, stepping into view, his pistol trained on the man. The man jumped at the sound and turned toward him, the blade catching momentarily between the door and the jamb. "Drop the knife and come towards me."

The man put his hands up, still holding the dagger, and he stepped slowly toward Hunter.

"I said drop the knife," Hunter repeated.

"Why don't you drop your gun?" the man said. *He's got balls*, Hunter thought.

"I think I'll respectfully decline," Hunter replied. Then, he repeated, even more firmly, "Drop the knife!" The man was only about ten feet away from him by now, his fingers twitching on the grip of the dagger.

I can't get arrested, Billy Liebermann thought. He already had a record. Tonight's murder and attempted B&E would surely put him in prison for life.

He knew he was quick, though. If he could just get close enough, maybe he could take this guy out, too. Then, fuck Elliot Logan. This hit was cursed from the start. Billy would just cut his losses and go home.

"Drop the knife," the man repeated in his good old boy accent. Billy was just a few feet away. Drop and lunge. That's all he had to do. And he was in range now.

In a flash, he bent his knees and dropped. He fully intended to jab the dagger into the man's abdomen. But in the fraction of a second before he died, he realized his mistake. The man had been holding the gun low, pointed toward Billy's stomach.

When he suddenly dropped, the man squeezed the trigger, and the bullet that would have entered his abdomen now entered his throat. Billy felt the blinding, choking pain as the bullet plowed through his throat, blowing out a chunk of skin and muscle in the back as it exited his neck at the base of his skull.

He felt himself hit the rough pavement of the parking lot, but he felt nothing after that.

Elliot jumped when he heard the gunshot. In that instant, he wondered if the Swift Pokers were not completely tied to the idea of stabbing. Did they use guns, too?

Elliot's usually large blue eyes were enormous now, the entire iris exposed as he paced wide-eyed around his apartment. His breathing was shallow, and he had to force himself to exhale and try to take a normal breath.

The shot was outside, but it hadn't entered his apartment, so he realized that it wasn't meant for him. Maybe it wasn't even a shot. Maybe it was just a car backfiring. Maybe he was in a panic for nothing.

Finally, he picked up his phone. Hunter was late.

When the buzzer of his intercom sounded, he jumped again, dropping his phone. He stumbled to the speaker at the side of his door and pressed the button.

"Hello?" he said with a quiver in his voice.

"Elliot, it's Hunter," he heard through the static. He pushed the buzzer unlocking the front door. He waited, listening. About fifteen seconds later, a knock sounded on his door and he looked through the peephole. Only when he saw Hunter did he unlock and open the door.

"Are you alright, son?" Hunter asked as he came in.

"Yeah, I'm okay. Are you? I thought I heard a gunshot."

"I'm fine. That was me. Your poker's dead out back."

Elliot exhaled heavily, realizing how close he had come. His legs felt weak and he collapsed into his chair.

"You're safe now, son," Hunter said soothingly. "It's over. Everything's alright now."

"Not yet," Elliot said.

I'm glad you're alright, Elliot," Valerie said as she held her phone out, the speaker turned on so Shannon could also hear. Hunter had gone out to the front of Elliot's building to talk to the police, but before he did, he had given Elliot Valerie's number.

"Me too," he replied. "I'm really lucky Hunter got here just in time."

It was a pleasant spring night, with just a bit of a chill, and a full moon overhead. Shannon and Valerie were walking along the creek that cut through the town and formed the diagonal back property line of their home. They were heading back, now, from the little bridge across the creek.

"But listen, there's more," continued Elliot's voice on the phone. "While I was waiting, I kept studying the code of the plug-in and found something else. Even though the plug-in suppresses the IP address of the computer it's operating on, and hides its location, it also works as a homing device for the owner, in case it gets lost or stolen.

"The person can use another device with the plug-in installed on it, as long as it has the same license number, to locate the missing computer. It pings its location when it's used. Kind of like a digital LoJack system for computers. So even though the detective took the computer, the last time you used it was at your home, and that's the location that was transmitted. The owner could be tracking its location."

"Oh my god, Elliot," Valerie said. "What the hell is wrong with these –" She was interrupted when Shannon roughly grabbed her shoulder, stopping her in her tracks. Shannon was staring ahead toward the front porch of their house.

Valerie turned and saw a man standing under the porch light. He had just knocked on their door and was waiting for someone to answer. Her first thought was that a little after eleven o'clock was quite late for a caller. But before she could say anything, Shannon clapped a hand over her mouth.

She took the phone out of Valerie's hand. "He's here now!" she whispered into it. "We have to go." She disconnected as Valerie turned her terrified gaze toward her. Shannon pulled her toward the shadows of a tree, punching the button to darken the screen of the phone.

"How do you know that's him?" Valerie asked in a frightened whisper.

"I saw his pictures on his Facebook profile when I first got the computer. That's him. Don something."

As they watched, the man glanced around, then threw his shoulder against the door, breaking it in. He was just stepping over the threshold when Valerie's phone rang.

Shannon jumped, dropping the phone, which immediately went dark and silent on the ground.

The man's head snapped in their direction.

"Run, Val!" Shannon said, still using an urgent whisper. They turned and raced north on Griffith Street, their shoes scuffing on the dirt road.

The man ran in their direction, hesitating for just a moment at his car, but as they were only about fifty yards ahead of him, he continued on foot. In the time it would take him to get in the car, start it up, back out and take off after them, they could find a hiding place and he could lose them.

Knowing they had to get out of his sight, Shannon turned left on 9th Street, dragging Valerie with her. As soon as they had rounded the corner, Shannon was scanning for places to hide. There was a bed and breakfast immediately on their right, but she figured the door would probably be locked this late.

When they got to Taos Street, they turned to the left again. Valerie glanced behind and saw the man rounding the corner on to 9th Street, only about a hundred and fifty feet behind them.

"Where are we going?" she whispered urgently.

"I don't know," Shannon shot back.

The small gothic stone structure of the First Presbyterian Church loomed on their left, a little bit of light shining out through the stained glass of its lancet windows. They ran around the square tower at the front toward the two sets of doors. Would it be open? Could it offer a place to hide? As

Valerie tried one set of doors and Shannon tried the other, they unhappily had their answer.

They continued running south on Taos, not knowing where they were going, but just trying to keep distance between them and their pursuer. They were both gasping for breath as they reached 6th Street. The town's main business district was on their right, The Happy Cooker on their left. The old fashioned street lamps were lit up, but nobody was around.

The little Police Department and Town Hall were to the left, just beyond The Happy Cooker, but they both knew the doors would be locked up.

"This way," Valerie said as she grabbed Shannon's hand and continued south across 6th Street.

Don Lewis hoped he was doing the right thing in chasing these two women. He assumed they were the ones who lived in that house, in which case they likely had damning information about him.

But it was also possible that they lived elsewhere, and had nothing to do with his computer. They had seen him break in the door, but could be unrelated to his mission, in which case he was wasting valuable time in chasing them. Time that he could be spending tossing the house for his computer.

But they had seen his face and his car, possibly even his license plate. Even if he retrieved his computer, he was still in danger of discovery. He could be identified. They had to be dealt with.

Two things seemed to be in his favor: They didn't appear to know where they were going, and nobody was out this late. Nice thing about small towns.

They had apparently stopped to try the doors at the church. He hadn't seen them do it, but he was closer to them when he rounded the corner.

But then they regained some distance when they ran flat out for two blocks. They were younger and more agile than he was.

His lungs were beginning to burn. With each pounding step, he felt the bulge of his pistol stuck in the back of his waistband. Under the full moon, and especially now, illuminated by the street lights, he knew he could easily take both of them down from here. But he didn't want the sound of the gunshots to draw attention to him before he was in a position to get away safely with his computer.

They hesitated briefly at what seemed to be the town's main street, but then they continued across it. If Lewis hadn't already been gasping, he would have sighed. He had to keep up. He couldn't let them get away.

Valerie and Shannon continued trudging down Taos Street, past the historic Hotel de Paris on their left. The way became more difficult when the pavement became rougher and they began climbing uphill. It was also darker, the only streetlight ahead at the corner of 4th Street.

When they reached 4th Street, they turned right, behind the bulk of the Georgetown Community School. Shannon threw herself against the clapboard wall of the building.

"I can't," she panted. Valerie went back to the corner and peeked around. Their pursuer was a couple of blocks behind, having at least as much trouble as they were.

"Okay, just a couple of seconds," Valerie wheezed, bending over and leaning her hands against her knees. She consciously tried to take slow, deep breaths, but her heart was pounding. She glanced around the corner again. He was just crossing 5th Street.

"Come on, honey," she said, "we have to go." Under the streetlight, she saw the imploring look on Shannon's face. "It's okay," Valerie encouraged, "it's downhill for a bit." She grabbed Shannon's hand and pulled her along, going west on 4th Street. It was indeed a little easier, going downhill, but on this block, 4th was little more than an alley, one that didn't actually go through to the next street.

They came up against a chain link fence, the street a few feet below, but Valerie saw a gate to the right. They went through it and down a short flight of wooden steps to the street level. As they went south on Rose Street, uphill again, Valerie glanced to her left, past the stone retaining wall they had just come down from, and saw their pursuer gaining on them.

By the time they crossed 3rd Street, they were moving barely faster than a fast walk. Their thighs were burning, their breath was rasping in their dry throats, and under the passing streetlight, Valerie saw black streaks on Shannon's face, tears washing her dark makeup down her cheeks.

They passed the intersection, Valerie dragging Shannon behind her. A few yards from the corner, she threw herself up the steps of a porch and against the door of a little clap-board-sided bungalow.

She pounded on the door, looking over her shoulder at the man coming after them. Despite his own struggle, he was only about fifty yards behind them. She could clearly see his angry, dogged expression as he got closer. She saw him reach a hand behind him, and when it reappeared, it was holding a gun.

Shannon was leaning back against the house, watching the man approach. She seemed more desperate to breathe than to escape. Her steady gaze at the man, and the black tears on her face, almost seemed to imply that she had re-signed herself to the impending outcome.

Valerie banged her fist repeatedly against the door, and her own tears began to flow.

Finally! Lewis thought. His lungs were burning, his heart was pounding, and his legs hadn't gotten a workout like that in years. He couldn't have taken much more. He really wished that he had taken the few extra seconds to get his car.

But at least the chase was over. Whether someone was home here or not, the end would be virtually the same. If nobody answered the door, he'd go ahead and finish them here. If somebody *was* home, it would actually be even bet-ter. He would force them inside and do all three of them, and being inside the house, the sound would be less likely to attract attention. It should be easy. People were always intimidated by a gun.

He slowed his pace and pulled it from his waistband.

He was only a few feet away now, and as he stood before the porch, wheezing, he looked them over. They were actually very good-looking women, although the dark-haired one was a little freaky. Still really pretty, though.

Shame.

When the porch light came on, Valerie gasped. She was still leaning against the door, so when it opened, she fell inside, against Tom Blevins, the Colorado Ranger. He put an arm around her.

"Valerie, what's wrong?" He looked up as Shannon turned and practically fell through the doorway herself. They were both panting and coughing, trying to catch their breath. Only then did he see the man just beyond them. He came up the last step onto the porch.

Tom watched, puzzled, as the man came across the threshold after them. He was gasping for breath, too.

"Who are you?" he asked. "What the hell's going on?" The man raised his right hand and Tom saw the gun. Tom tried to move Valerie behind him, putting himself into a protective position in front of her. The man, apparently confident due to his possession of a gun, turned slightly to close the door. That's when Tom raised his own gun and pointed it at the man. He saw surprise register on the man's face.

"What?" Tom said. "I hear frantic pounding on my door in the night, and you think I'm not going to come prepared? Drop it."

So it's my fault you almost got killed!" Elliot said. "I didn't hear what you whispered in the phone, and I thought we just got cut off. If I hadn't called you back, he never would have chased you." He looked at Valerie. "And your phone wouldn't have broken."

"Yeah, it's all your fault," Shannon replied. "I'm the one who stole the fucking computer and got that son of a bitch coming after us in the first place, but we almost got killed just because you called to see if we were okay. You bastard!" She looked at him coyly, softening her remarks with a smile. "You're so full of shit."

"Honey, not so loud," Valerie said as she looked around the Panera Bread.

They had agreed to meet here late the next morning, after they had gotten some sleep. It was also late in the morning to allow Hunter time to meet with the FBI. And for them to drive from Georgetown to northeast Denver.

Valerie would have thought that the FBI office would be downtown. Instead, it was located in a sprawling building on East 36th Avenue, in the part of town where the old Stapleton International Airport used to be.

Shannon looked at Valerie. Her first inclination was to sneer at her and remark that she needs to 'chill the fuck out.' But in the last twenty-four hours, she had developed a deeper bond with her aunt. Her resolve the evening before, to be better family to Valerie, kept coming to the front of her mind.

Especially after Valerie's encouragement and quick thinking last night had saved their lives. Shannon hadn't known where to go. She was just running blindly away. But Valerie had thought to run to where her Ranger friend lived.

After Don Lewis had been arrested, Tom Blevins turned his attention to the two of them. Especially to Valerie. Shannon could see that there was something there, with him, anyway. He was glad he had been there and able to help, but he seemed genuinely sorry that Valerie still, apparently, did not return his affection.

Now, after having lingered over coffee and breakfast for nearly an hour, Hunter walked in the door. He saw them and waved, then went to the counter to get a cup of coffee. He was seated with them in just a couple of minutes.

"Well," he said, "it turns out they don't need to see you guys just yet. They'll be talking to you over the next couple of days, but my report was all they needed to get the ball rolling. I'm sorry I had you come all the way out here."

"It's okay, Hunter," Valerie said. "We're happy to do it. I appreciate everything you and Elliot have done for us."

Elliot, aware of the delay he created by not believing Shannon, was anxious to deflect the conversation.

"So what's the FBI doing?" he asked.

"I gave them the laptop that we found in Detective Hardison's car, and told them what you told me about that plug-in thingamajig. They're going to be looking at that, but the first thing they already got going was a subpoena being issued to Facebook. They're out in Menlo Park, California, though, so the California FBI is handling that part.

"But they'll be able to get all the names and locations of the members of the Swift Poker group, and in the next day or two, there'll be tons of arrests made around the country. They're conducting it quietly and won't be scheduling any press conferences about it until after they have it contained.

"They wanted me to stress to y'all not to say anything about it either. Stealth is as important as speed in getting everybody involved."

They all nodded in agreement.

"Yeah, I think I'm kind of Facebooked out for a while," Shannon said.

"So, these were just a bunch of angry people who banded together?" Valerie asked.

"Apparently," Hunter replied. "Facebook is cooperating fully. From what we've learned already through preliminary conversations with them, a lot of the members seem to be bigots, others are spurned lovers like Elliot mentioned to me last night. Some of the posts in the group were political rants, racist remarks, gay bashing, you name it. And these people banded together to do their part to try to rid the world of these so-called undesirables.

"They were all sworn to secrecy. And pending further investigation, it appears that a few members who apparently experienced qualms of conscience were dealt with in much the same way as their other victims. That's only suspected at this point, though."

"That's awful!" Valerie said.

"Yeah, it is," Hunter agreed, taking a sip of his coffee. "If you think about it, though, it's kind of scarier when you think about all the people with these kinds of hang-ups who haven't organized. They're walking among us, just waiting for something to make them snap. Hopefully they won't, but we've seen it happen too many times."

"So what's on your agenda, now?" Valerie asked.

"Well, I've offered my services and expertise to the FBI to assist in their investigation. Whether they take me up on it remains to be seen." He looked at his watch. "But for now, I think I might drive down to Cherry Creek and take my honey out to lunch." Valerie smiled and finished the last of her coffee.

"Do you like Evanescence?" Elliot asked Shannon.

"I *love* Evanescence!" she replied.

"I have a bootleg video of a concert they did a couple of years ago, if you'd like to see it."

"Bootleg?" she asked. She glanced at Valerie, then back at Elliot. "I've kind of given up on my illegal activities, so let's just call it an unofficial alternative venue." She smiled at him. "But I'd love to see it."

Hunter pulled up in front of Zephyr Fine Art Gallery where Kenzie was waiting for him. She was easy to spot, her red hair blazing like shiny copper in the sun directly overhead.

She got in the car and leaned over to kiss him. He noticed the tears in her eyes.

"Hey," he said, "what's wrong, baby?"

She hesitated for a moment before opening up.

"We can go," she said, motioning that he didn't have to stay parked. He put the car in gear and pulled into traffic. "Sunday, at the barbecue," Kenzie continued, "JuleighAnn told me that Jim had contacted her and asked her to have me call him. I figured it was about divorce papers, which I know I need to take care of. But I procrastinated because I just didn't want any contact with him.

"Well, I finally worked up the nerve this morning. I called him during my mid-morning break, figuring that the conversation would have to be short and civil." She paused and took a deep breath. "Lainey died."

"That's his sister?" Hunter asked. He had heard a little about Lainey.

"Yes, my friend with multiple sclerosis. Well, a couple of weeks ago, the MS finally won."

"Aw, honey, I'm sorry."

As Kenzie's marriage to Jim deteriorated, Lainey, motivated by her guilt about having brought them together, and exacerbated by the disease, started apologizing to her every time she saw her. The visits often ended in tears and depression, and Kenzie, feeling morose herself, gradually slacked off in her visits.

Approximately three years ago, as the disease progressed, Lainey's family had finally placed her in a facility that was better able to administer the ongoing care she needed. In that setting, the visits became even harder for Kenzie, and they all but ceased.

She thought about Lainey often, and felt guilty about abandoning her. But her own life had become so painful that the sad visits just compounded her own depression.

Over the last couple of days, remembering her friendship with Lainey, Kenzie had resolved that she was going to reconnect with her.

And now she was gone forever.

That evening, Hunter drove Kenzie to the Stewarts' house.

"It still looks exactly the same," she remarked as they pulled up in front of the house. Hunter was accommodating, putting his arm around her frequently, holding her hand. "It feels weird," she continued, "coming here and knowing that Lainey's not here anymore."

"Do you want me to wait out here," Hunter asked, "or come in with you?"

"I want you with me," Kenzie replied, "if you feel up to it. Jim's not here, and the Stewarts are really sweet."

"You got it, baby," he said as he pulled himself out of the car. Kenzie didn't wait for him to open her door, but he was on her side by the time she got out. He walked beside her toward the front door, his hand gently on the small of her back, just to let her know he was there.

The front door opened before they climbed the steps, and Jill Stewart greeted Kenzie, her arms, and her smile, wide. Engulfed in her arms, Kenzie's tears started flowing.

"Oh sweetie," Jill said, "it's okay. She's not suffering anymore. And it's not like it came unexpectedly."

"I know," Kenzie sniffed. "But it's fresh to me. I just found out about it."

"Yeah, I know, sweetie." Jill quietly smiled at Hunter over Kenzie's shoulder, but gave Kenzie time to regain her composure.

"Jill," Kenzie finally said, pulling away from her, "this is Hunter Sage." She put her arm through his, and Hunter extended his right hand.

"Very nice to meet you, ma'am," he said as she shook his hand. "And I'm very sorry for your loss."

"Thank you, Hunter. And it's nice to meet you, too. Come on in, both of you."

They went inside and Kenzie immediately felt at home, being in the house where she had spent so much of her late teens and early twenties.

"It still looks the same," she said. "Except it doesn't seem quite right without Lainey here."

Jill's husband came into the living room, also with a smile on his face.

"I thought I heard voices in here," he said, and Kenzie happily received his hug as well.

"Jack, this is Hunter Sage," she said, quick to include Hunter. "Hunter, Jack Stewart."

"Jack and Jill," Hunter said with a smile and a handshake.

"Yes," Jill said, smiling back. "And Jimmy Stewart. We're a pun family."

"Sit down, sit down," Jack insisted. "Make yourselves comfortable. Would you like anything to drink?"

"No, thank you, Jack," Kenzie replied as she and Hunter settled on the sofa. "We really can't stay long. Jim just told me that I needed to see you both. And once I learned about Lainey, I *wanted* to see you. I wanted to apologize for abandoning her. And you."

"You don't need to apologize," Jill said. Jack left the room as Jill was talking, with a gesture that said he'd be right back. "It certainly wasn't easy," Jill continued. "The MS changed her. She just wasn't the same sweet girl she used to be."

"I know, but I just feel like such a fair weather friend. Things got tough and I stopped coming around."

"Honey, I know what it was like," Jill said sympathetically. "It wasn't just Lainey, but Jimmy, too. I know he became harder to deal with after getting injured and losing out on that shot with the New England Patriots. You had your hands full with him."

"Stop being so nice," Kenzie said insistently, but with a smile. Jill smiled affectionately back at her.

Jack came back into the room, carrying something in front of him. Kenzie recognized the old blanket that Lainey had used to cover her works in progress.

"Lainey had several pieces that she had carved on her own, without commission," Jim said as he placed the object on the coffee table. "Over the years, she would donate them to different organizations. She donated a tiger and a lion to the Wild Animal Sanctuary up northeast of Denver. She donated a carving of a couple of playing puppies to the Denver Dumb Friends League.

"But this one, she worked at for several years, off and on, depending on how she was feeling. Even after the MS took hold pretty hard, she'd be out there working on a little portion of this a few minutes at a time, for as long as she could.

"She didn't quite get it finished, but her wishes were that it go to you." With that, he reached over and lifted the blanket off of the dark walnut carving of a long-haired dachshund, sitting up as tall as its stubby little legs would allow. From where it sat on the table, it was looking directly at Kenzie, its head tilted a bit to one side.

Kenzie's eyes instantly filled with tears when she saw it.

"Aw, Strudel," she said. Peripherally, she could sense Hunter looking toward her. "She was a long-haired dachshund I had when I was growing up," she explained.

She leaned forward to examine the carving more closely. The workmanship was impeccable, the expression on the face sweet and adorable. Overall, it was typical Lainey.

Kenzie could see, toward the bottom and primarily in the back, where the carving of the fur was not as smooth and finished as elsewhere. Lainey had focused her attention on the main features first, getting them finished and refined, before expending energy on the less important parts. Knowing her, Kenzie thought, she likely wanted to finish the head and face perfectly, just in case she wasn't able to finish the rest of the piece.

With the tears now tumbling silently down her cheeks, Kenzie looked at the Stewarts and smiled. "It looks just like Strudel," she said.

"Lainey knew how much you loved that dog," Jack said with a nod. "She started this project especially for you."

"Bless you, Lainey," Kenzie said under her breath.

On the way back home, with Strudel covered again and strapped into the back seat, Kenzie was thinking.

"You know, I'll bet it would be really easy to get Zephyr interested in a posthumous Lainey Stewart exhibit."

"Are there enough pieces for an exhibit?" Hunter asked.

"Jack said they still have a few," Kenzie replied slowly, allowing the idea to take shape in her mind. "And there's Strudel. And I could talk to some of the people and organizations she sold and donated to. I'm sure I can round up several who would be willing to loan their pieces just for the length of an exhibit."

"Honey, I think that'd be really nice. She was certainly a gifted artist. That would be a beautiful tribute, to direct some attention to her talent."

"I think I'll talk to my boss about it tomorrow. I should probably take Strudel with me, to show her the kind of work that Lainey did."

Hunter smiled, giving Kenzie the quiet she needed to formulate her idea. After a few minutes, as they neared their home, Kenzie broke the silence.

"I think I just want to go to bed," she said.

"Now you're talking," Hunter replied. "That sounds really good. Especially since I walked out on you last night."

"Oh yeah," Kenzie said. "What was that about?"

Hunter briefly considered telling her about the man with the knife who tried to kill him, but who was instead killed by Hunter.

He immediately decided against it.

"Nothing nearly as interesting as you, baby girl," he said.

Penn finished packing his bag and zipped it up. He put it down on the floor, next to the door of the guest suite, and decided to do one last walk-through of the bedroom and the bathroom. He didn't find anything that he had forgotten.

He stopped at the window and looked out across the lake. From here, he could see part of the deck below, where he and Valerie had first met. Was it really only five days ago? Then, farther out, outside the fence, he saw the spot where she had slipped on the muddy shore and he had caught her, holding her in his arms for a moment.

Their relationship didn't have an easy beginning, but knowing what little he did about her history, he was starting to understand it a little better. They had chatted a few times on Facebook since then, and that did seem to help. Valerie appeared to feel comfortable being herself when she was online.

After a bit of coaxing, Penn had even talked her into dinner last night. The fact that JuleighAnn offered to cook dinner for them seemed to help. Valerie was comfortable around JuleighAnn and Arden. So a relaxed, casual, home-cooked dinner here was easier for Valerie to accept. As enamored as Penn was with Valerie, he was happy for all the help he could get.

It had been a good evening. Valerie hadn't said much about what she had been up to this week, but she did open up a little about her history, giving Penn greater insight into the reason for her hang-ups. And he was crazy enough about her that her hang-ups didn't even matter to him.

He leaned a shoulder against the side of the window frame, looking out at the lake. Several varieties of ducks were gathered in various groupings across the water and, as he had done numerous times during the past week, Penn was transfixed by them. They were so calming.

He remembered his view of the Charles River from his fourth floor studio. It was nice. He loved the view, but it was a city view. Brownstones, city streets, and Cambridge across the river. But here, despite the suburban neighborhood around it, was a wild view. Natural.

Valerie's description of where she lived sounded even more so. He had told her last night that he would come again, and when he did, he wanted to see where she lived.

"I'd like that," she had said. He smiled as he remembered her saying that. "I'd like that." It seemed to echo in his memory, and each time he heard it, it never failed to warm his heart.

"There she is," Arden said as he twisted around, looking out the front window.

"Who?" Penn asked.

"Oh, did I forget to tell you?" Arden had a mischievous look on his face, one which Penn had become accustomed to in his week here. "Valerie offered to drive you to the airport."

Penn felt his heart race a bit, and he stood up in anticipation of her entry. He felt like a teenager waiting for his prom date to make her appearance. Arden opened the front door before she had a chance to ring the bell.

She greeted Arden, and JuleighAnn who was resting in her recliner after an unusually busy day of multiple hospital visits. Valerie turned to Penn and gave him a warm gaze and a soft smile.

Penn shook his head slightly as he looked at her, amazed at the effect she had on him. He knew she wasn't an *actual* angel. He knew she didn't *really* glow with a soft, golden light. He knew she wasn't *absolutely* perfect.

That was just silly.

Yet, that's the way he saw her.

"Valerie," he said, "what a nice surprise."

"Surprise?" she replied, puzzled. "Didn't Arden tell you I was going to drive you?"

"He did. Just now."

"Sounds like him," she said as she walked past Arden, giving him a scolding look out the corner of her eye. Arden smiled, unaffected. Valerie stepped forward and gave Penn a quick, unassuming kiss. Not satisfied with just that, Penn wrapped his arms around her and held her tightly, and he sighed when he felt her arms close around him in return. Only after giving her a kiss on the side of her neck, then her cheek, then finally her lips, did he let her go.

JuleighAnn, still sprawled out on her recliner, watched them for a moment and smiled. Then she looked past them at Arden.

Their eyes locked, and they each exchanged a warm gaze and a soft smile.

It was mid afternoon on Friday, before the rush hour, so traffic was light for the forty minute trip to the airport. Penn was happy to be able to spend the time with Valerie, but sad that soon, he was going to leave her behind.

They chatted idly on the way, and Penn marveled at how quickly he had fallen for her. He had spent more time with Arden during the past week than with anybody else, seeing all the touristy sights. Yet this quiet, beautiful, messed up woman had made the greatest impression on him.

He wasn't entirely sure of her feelings for him. Arden and JuleighAnn both confirmed that she had opened up to his advances more than any other man they had witnessed. That was encouraging. But to Penn, Valerie still seemed to be hiding behind her walls. To an extent, at least.

He did notice the looks that she would cast at him from time to time, as if she were trying to figure something out herself. Those times he caught her looking at him, it usually resulted in a somewhat embarrassed smile between them. Often, he would take her hand, and every time, their fingers interlocked tightly.

He was holding her hand now, in fact, as she drove, his thumb gently caressing the back of her hand. He was looking down at her slim fingers curled between his, wishing they could stay like this.

Then he felt her eyes on him and looked up at her, just as she looked back at the road. He wished he knew what she was thinking, wished he knew how to ask her without sounding needy or intrusive. God, why did he have to be so damned sensitive?

The barren landscape was becoming more punctuated with airport-related buildings and services, and Penn knew that his minutes with Valerie were numbered, especially when he saw the white tent tops of Denver International Airport growing larger.

Valerie felt Penn's gentle caress on her hand, and she was confused. How did she ever get to this point? All those years she had carefully and resolutely pushed men away. Yet now, in less than a week, she had allowed this one to breach the walls she had built around her heart.

The week had been distracting, to say the least, what with Shannon's poking fiasco on Facebook and with them almost getting killed. With samples from opposite ends of the emotional scale, and various points in between, it's no wonder she felt confused.

On the other hand, maybe it was almost getting killed that had opened her heart to love. Life is short and could end at any time. What a shame it would be to die alone, with nobody to share those fleeting moments with.

Was Penn the one? She didn't know. After all these years, she wasn't even sure how to tell anymore. But he was certainly a sweet and gentle soul. Even Shannon liked him.

She thought about how easily Shannon had connected with Elliot. He asked her if she wanted to watch a bootleg video, she said yes, and they were engaged in watching it when Valerie left to pick up Penn.

Why couldn't it be that easy for Valerie? Why did she always seem to second-guess everyone, including herself? Or question motives? Why did she have to be so sensitive?

Their conversation had quieted in the last few minutes, each of them immersed in their own thoughts. Valerie envied Penn. He seemed so calm and together. With the white tent roof of the airport looming, he was fine. He didn't seem tense or in turmoil like she was.

Valerie followed the signs to the West Terminal and drove in where it said "Departures." There were several signs for United, and she pulled up to the curb at the first opening.

Penn looked at her for a moment before pulling his hand from hers. He got out and opened the back door, wrestled his bag out and placed it on the sidewalk. He looked back into the car, but Valerie wasn't in her seat. He spun around and found her standing next to him.

She smiled at him, and took his hand.

"It was nice meeting you and getting to know you," she said, cringing as she did at how cold and formal the statement sounded.

"Yes, it was *very* nice," Penn agreed. "This was just what I needed. A nice, relaxing few days away."

A nice, relaxing few days? Valerie and Shannon's run across Georgetown the other night flashed across her mind, but she dismissed it.

"I'm sorry I'm not the easiest person to get to know," she said. "I tend to pick people apart and push them away."

"I tend to pull people to me and *then* pick them apart," Penn replied. "Or just bore them to death."

"Are you kidding? I don't think you're boring at all. I enjoyed our time together, when I could get past my own neuroses." She chuckled. "And here I was thinking you had it all together."

"Ah," Penn smiled, "so you haven't yet seen past my carefully constructed façade." He gazed into her eyes, wishing he could get lost in them, as an excuse to stay. "I guess I'm not that easy to get to know, either."

Valerie smiled back at him, feeling her misgivings of a few moments ago weaken a bit.

"Well, we still have a few years ahead of us," she said. "I guess we have time to learn how."

Penn allowed his eyes to travel over her face, memorizing her features. Then, impulsively, he swept her into his arms, burying his left hand in her golden hair, supporting her head as he pressed his lips against hers. Her body molded itself against his, and she wrapped her arms around him, feeling her insecurities relax a bit, even as her body tensed.

245

Too soon, their lips parted, but their eyes locked inches apart, their hearts racing, pounding against each other.

"Boston, huh?" Valerie said, barely over a whisper.

"It's a nice place," Penn replied, hopefully. "Although I think I could get used to Colorado. This week has shown me what's been missing in my life."

"Oh yeah? What's that?"

"You."

Valerie shook her head slightly, her eyes clouding with tears.

"Call me when you get home," she said.

"I hope you're prepared to hear from me every day," he replied.

"If I don't, I'll be calling you," Valerie smiled. "Although, in time, that could get expensive."

Penn pulled away and extended the handle on his suitcase.

"Well," he said thoughtfully, "Facebook, then. That's always safe."

Kenzie pushed the clothes aside and poked around through the boxes on the floor of the hall closet. She hadn't realized what a mess it already was, after only living here a few months.

There didn't seem to be any rhyme or reason to it. Some of the stuff was Hunter's, some was hers, and the boxes were just stuffed in there, apparently, based on the size of the box and the size of the hole it was filling.

She was sure she still had it. She clearly remembered packing it up when she moved away from Jim and went to North Carolina. Then, when moving back to Colorado, she was debating whether to move it again or not. Hunter encouraged her to keep it.

That brief thought of Jim reminded her of her short talk with him the other day. He had actually been quite civil. She had been right about divorce papers. He had gotten started on them a while back and then let it wait until he contacted her.

The divorce would be simple. He had even asked her if she wanted maintenance or not, which she declined. She now had a copy of the papers to look over and sign.

She didn't know what had caused the change in him. Maybe he realized that it was his behavior that had made Kenzie leave him, and he recognized he was in the wrong. Maybe it was Lainey dying that mellowed him out. Whatever it was, Kenzie was grateful that she didn't have to deal with a disgruntled or angry ex-husband on top of Lainey's death.

She didn't find what she was looking for, and she closed up the closet. She stood there thinking for a moment. Maybe in the office closet.

She went into the office where Jarvis was dozing in a patch of late afternoon sunlight on the carpet. He lazily lifted his head and looked when Kenzie opened the closet door, then put his head back down.

There were a couple of boxes here, and when she opened the larger one, she saw what she was looking for. She tugged it out of the closet and began digging through her old art supplies. She took out a sketch pad first of all. Rummaging a little more, she found several tubes of paint, most of them hardened from the years of disuse. She would have to replace them.

But she was determined. She remembered what Lainey had told her at their first meeting, just after she had criticized Kenzie's painting: "Someone who can paint this beautifully must be able to see wonderful things!"

"Yes, I can, Lainey," she said.

She knew she was sadly out of practice, but she would get it back. Lainey had faith in her, faith which Kenzie herself had been lacking for so long.

Tomorrow, she decided, she would go out and buy new paint. Probably some new brushes, too. And she would need some canvases.

But for now, she would start sketching. She took her sketch pad and a pencil and sat down at the desk. She opened the pad to a blank page and looked at it. The clean, white paper was intimidating. The image in her mind was so vivid, but transferring it to the paper was the hard part. Especially since Kenzie had never worked strictly from imagination before.

Before she started feeling too daunted by what she was determined to do, she put a mark on the page. She followed that with another, then another. The graphite lines began to take shape.

She roughly blocked in the dark hair, the ever-present smile, the twinkling eyes. She remembered Lainey's face so vividly, and though the features weren't exactly accurate, Kenzie captured her friend's exuberant happiness and her kind and bubbly personality.

"Oh, you found it," Hunter said as he came in the office. He placed a glass of chardonnay on the desk near Kenzie, and he took a sip of his Jack Daniels as he looked over her shoulder.

"Thank you," Kenzie said as she sipped the wine. "Yes, I found it, but I think I've lost it."

"What do you mean?"

"It's been so long since I've actually done my own artwork that I'm afraid any talent I might have had has evaporated by now."

"Oh, I don't know about that, sugarpie. I mean, I didn't know Lainey, but it looks like you got all her features in the right place."

Kenzie looked up at him, and then smiled when she realized that he was making a joke.

"It just doesn't quite look like her," Kenzie said.

"Well, you know what?" Hunter said as he sat down in the arm chair. "Considering it's been, what? Fifteen years? I'd say that looks damn good!"

"But I want to be able to make it look like her. She deserves a good portrait."

"And she'll have one. Honey, you're an artist. You were born with talent. But after all this time, you're out of practice. You just have to hone that talent and refine it again."

"I never listened to Lainey when she encouraged me like that. What makes you think you'll be successful where she failed?" Kenzie asked facetiously.

"You like my lovin'," he said. Kenzie snorted.

"Okay, I'm busy here," Kenzie said. "Don't be cute."

"Sugar, I'm stuck with this cuteness. There ain't no switch I can flip to turn it off." He took another sip of Jack as Kenzie shook her head. "Besides," he continued, "a good portrait shows the person's soul. From what you told me about Lainey, I'd say you've already captured that. Just practice a little, and it'll be perfect."

Kenzie regarded him for several moments.

"I love you, Hunter," she said softly.

"Aw, you know I love you too, honey."

With her work schedule that week, combined with Penn's visit, JuleighAnn had no choice but to leave *Green Eyed Lady* lying neglected on her bedside table. Now that they had the house to themselves again, she was determined to finish it.

Not that it was that good. It was one of the most absurd stories she had ever read, certainly a tribute to Arden's warped sense of humor.

During the course of the story, the hero, Augustine, had fought with a ruthless band of backwoods hicks straight out of *Deliverance*, and with "evil medieval knights." He had battled a dragon and been abducted by aliens, using his quick wit to talk his way out of an anal probe.

Sometimes it seemed as if Arden employed symbolism. The account involving the dragon, for instance, reminded JuleighAnn of what she knew about Evelyn, his ex-wife. And the account with the cast of *Deliverance* sounded a lot like his run-in with a violent biker, although Arden didn't come out quite as unscathed in real life.

Really, one of the stupidest things she had read. But it was Arden's gift to her, and she had to know how it ended.

As Arden worked on an art job in his office, JuleighAnn took the book downstairs to the family room and stretched out on the sofa.

> Augustine Smith trudged up the hill, blood-stained and exhausted, dragging his broadsword behind him. Once he attained the crest, he surveyed his surroundings. His enemies had been vanquished. They all lay dead at his feet, scattered in all directions, slain single-handedly by Augustine's super-human strength and his unusually shrewd battle planning.
>
> Only one thing he needed now. His sweetiepie, Gillian, she of the viridian orbs.
>
> Except that he knew she was peculiarly persnickety about blood and filth and stink. Maybe he should take one of his lavender and chamomile bubble baths first.
>
> Well, he was pretty hungry, too. He could really use a Chipotle's barbacoa burrito.
>
> And a nap.
>
> Maybe he should see Gillian tomorrow.

The story went on like that for a few more pages, as Gus got cleaned up. He put on clean clothes, combed some "smell-um" through his hair, and then took off on his mighty steed, a Budweiser Clydesdale, to meet up with Gillian.

JuleighAnn was nearing the end of the book as Augustine finally gained access to the object of his desire. Gillian lived in a gingerbread castle on a lake. Aside from the gingerbread, it was pretty easy to draw the correct conclusion.

> Augustine Smith felt his pulse quicken as the lady Gillian approached.
>
> "Thou hast traveled far," she said, "and battled hard, good knight."
>
> "Good night," he replied.
>
> "No, Gus, I am complimenting thee on the successful completion of thy travails."
>
> "Ah, thank you, milady."
>
> "I hereby grant thee rest and respite, that thou canst verily relish peaceful repose and commodious tranquility."
>
> "Huh?"
>
> "Take a little time off and get thy groove on."
>
> "You're most gracious, milady."
>
> She hesitated when he lingered before her.
>
> "Is there more, good knight?" she asked.
>
> "Good n – uh, yes," he replied. "There is something of the utmost importance that I must communicate to you."

At this point, the story ended. This was the last page, and JuleighAnn was confused. The story wasn't wrapped up by any means.

She inspected the book a little more closely and noticed that the last page seemed to have been torn out. Feeling frustrated that she wouldn't be able to finish reading it after all, she climbed the stairs and went into Arden's office. He looked up from his computer when she walked in, and he noticed the disappointment on her face.

"What's the matter, buckaroo?" he asked.

"Looks like whoever printed this screwed up," she replied. "The last page was torn out."

Arden took the book from her and looked at it, making a prolonged display of turning pages back and forth, as if that would supply the answer. Finally, he handed it back to her.

"You're right. It looks like it's been torn out."

"Yeah, that's what I said," JuleighAnn replied in an irritated tone, scrunching her eyebrows together.

Arden turned to the side and pulled open the lower drawer in his desk. He rummaged through some papers before pulling out one sheet. It was the size of a page from the book, with one torn edge.

"See if this one fits," he said. She took it from him, casting a lingering look of puzzlement at him. Then she turned and looked at the page.

> "Please," Gillian said, "do state thy important utterance."
>
> "Well, milady," Gus began, "you're, without exception, the finest and sweetest woman I've ever had the pleasure to know."

254

"I am," she agreed. "Go on."

"So, a quality woman like yourself should be joined with the finest man *you've* ever known."

"And where would I find such a towering figure of a man?"

"Kneeling before you, milady," Gus replied. "Will you marry me?"

And that was where it ended. While she was reading, JuleighAnn hadn't noticed that Arden had moved. But when she turned back to him, he was down on one knee, holding a diamond ring in front of him.

Fully intending to ream him for the still unfinished ending, she gasped when she realized what he was doing.

"JuleighAnn," he said, "when you look at me, your eyes see the man I want to be. And I know I have a better chance of becoming that man when I'm with you, since you inspire me in so many ways."

Her hand on her chest, JuleighAnn stood as motionless as if she were carved from marble. She kept holding her breath and she had to remind herself to exhale.

"I'm touched by your warm and generous heart in ways I've never been touched before. I'm challenged by your intelligence, because you make me see things in a new way. I'm captivated by the depths of your soul, as you daily draw me in to the essence of your being. And I'm arrested by your love, my heart imprisoned in the sweet, gentle confinement of your benevolent nature."

JuleighAnn was particularly focusing on what Arden was saying. She could no longer see him clearly, as she looked at him through the tears in her eyes.

"Honey, in the time I've known you, I've found that making you happy is the primary thing in my life that makes *me* happy. I'll be the happiest man in the world if you will agree to be my wife, because I promise to spend the rest of my life making *you* happy.

"JuleighAnn Harper, will you marry me?"

JuleighAnn smiled, sending the tears slipping down her cheeks. She looked down at Arden, at his smiling, expectant face, and she took his hand.

"Imprisoned?" she said. "Confinement? That's the best you could come up with?"

Arden opened his mouth to say something, but couldn't think of what to say. His eyes darted back and forth, apparently in something of a panic, then he looked back at JuleighAnn's face. Her smile was even broader now.

"Of course I'll marry you, my love," she said.

Arden stood up, sighing with relief, and slipped the ring on her finger. He took her in his arms and kissed her, tenderly at first, then more passionately. With her recent shallow respirations, JuleighAnn was having a hard time with the lengthy kiss and pushed Arden away, panting.

"Thou taketh my breath away, good knight," she said.

"Good night," Arden said, and he buried his face in her hair.